Best Friends Are Forever.

The bedroom door burst open. Becka dropped her knitting. Lilah sat up straight. Trish leapt to her feet.

All three of them stared in surprise as a girl with a mane of long auburn hair excitedly swept into the room.

"Becka!" the girl cried. She threw her arms around Becka and wrapped her in a tight hug. "Becka! Becka! I'm so happy to see you!" she squealed.

"I can't believe it!" the girl cried. "I just can't believe it! Becka—it's you! It's really *you!*"

Becka gasped, utterly speechless. Who *is* this girl? she asked herself.

I've never seen her before!

Don't miss these chilling tales from

FEAR STREET®

After hours, the horror continues at

FEAR STREET® NIGHTS

R.L. STINE

FEAR STREET®

THE BEST FRIEND

Simon Pulse
New York London Toronto Sydney

A Parachute Press book

SIMON PULSE
An imprint of Simon & Schuster Children's Publishing Division
1230 Avenue of the Americas, New York, NY 10020
Copyright © 1992 by Parachute Publishing, L.L.C.
All rights reserved, including the right of reproduction in whole or in part in any form.
SIMON PULSE and colophon are registered trademarks of
Simon & Schuster, Inc.
FEAR STREET is a registered trademark of Parachute Press, Inc.
Designed by Sammy Yuen Jr.
The text of this book was set in Times.
Manufactured in the United States of America
This Simon Pulse edition April 2006
10 9
Library of Congress Control Number 2005929887
ISBN-13: 978-1-4169-1376-4
ISBN-10: 1-4169-1376-9

THE BEST FRIEND

chapter
1

"Ow—stop. You're hurting me!"

Eric Fraser loosened his grip on Becka Norwood's shoulders. "Sorry. I didn't mean to." His face reddened. He stared at the snow-covered windshield.

Becka slid away from him until her shoulder bumped the car door. She adjusted the collar of her coat.

Why am I sitting here kissing him? she thought. I'm going to break up with him.

Big, wet snowflakes continued to fall. The windows were completely blanketed now. It's like being inside an igloo, Becka thought, shivering.

Turning his dark eyes to hers, Eric leaned forward, reaching for her.

She raised her arm to block him. "We have to talk," she said, not meaning to sound shrill.

"Talk?" He giggled for some reason. Becka realized that she hated his giggle. It always burst out at the wrong time.

He stretched his arm around her shoulders and tried to pull her closer.

"No. Really," she insisted, twisting to get out from under his arm.

He acted hurt. "What do you want to talk about?"

Becka chewed the tip of her thumb, a nervous habit.

Here goes, she thought. Her stomach felt feathery. Her throat tightened.

She realized she always felt jumpy around Eric. They'd been dating since school started in September. More than three months. But she never felt comfortable with him.

He was so . . . so needy.

She stopped chewing her thumb, clasped her hands together in her lap. "I think we need to talk about—things." It was cold in the car, parked beside the woods, the engine off, no heater. She shivered again.

Eric rolled his eyes. "Why do you always want to talk?" His voice revealed more than impatience. He sounded angry.

"Why don't you *ever* want to talk?" she demanded. Her voice trembled. The feathers in her stomach turned to stone.

Don't cry, she instructed herself, biting her lower, lip.

It's not the end of the world. You're just breaking up with him. You haven't even been going out with him that long.

He turned away from her and gripped the steering wheel with both hands. "Why are you on my case?" he asked. "You said you wanted to come here."

"I know."

"So why do you want to start a fight? I said I was

2

sorry. About holding your shoulder too tight. It was an accident." He ran a hand back through his short, brown hair, smoothing it.

Becka's heart was pounding. She shifted uncomfortably in the seat. Outside, the wind roared, piling more snow up against the windshield.

Don't cry, she told herself again.

Be cool. For once in your life, be cool.

"I think we shouldn't go out anymore." There. I said it.

"Huh?"

She turned to see his startled expression.

"You heard me."

He giggled. That hideous, inappropriate giggle again. He moved his hands on the steering wheel, circling them around and around.

"I think we should start seeing other people," Becka added, her voice shaking.

Don't cry.

"Okay," he said. His face became a blank—no expression at all. "No problem."

She suddenly felt she had to explain. "I think you're a great guy, Eric, but—"

He raised a hand to stop her. His expression remained a blank. "I said no problem. I'll take you home, Becka."

He raised the collar of his leather bomber jacket. Then he turned the key in the ignition. The car hesitated a second before starting up.

He's certainly being cool about this, Becka thought, chewing the end of her thumb and staring straight ahead.

I'm a nervous wreck.

You're *always* a nervous wreck, she told herself.

If only her heart would stop pounding so hard. She could feel her pulse throb at her temples.

He switched on the wipers. They pushed the light fresh snow off the windshield, allowing the blackness of the night to fill the car. The headlights cut a tunnel through the darkness, illuminating the large, falling flakes.

"I'm sorry—" Becka started.

"No problem," Eric repeated. He lowered his foot on the gas pedal, and the car slid out onto the snow-covered road.

Does he have to keep saying that?

He doesn't seem hurt at all, Becka thought, more than a little disappointed.

She had hoped it would go easily. But not *this* easily.

She didn't want a fight.

It seemed that they'd done nothing but fight for weeks. Every discussion turned into a fight. Every time they went out, they found themselves arguing. Or just bickering.

That was one reason Becka decided to break up with Eric.

Bill Planter was the other reason.

She had no intention of bringing up Bill tonight.

Staring out at the silent, falling snow, Becka thought about Bill. She wondered where he was, what he was doing.

Maybe I'll drive over to his house in the Old Village, she thought. Just drop in on him. Mention that I broke up with Eric.

No. No way. Forget that idea.

Her parents would murder her if they even suspected she was thinking about dating Bill again. They were so relieved, so grateful when Becka had dumped Bill and started going out with Eric.

But Eric was so immature. Always picking fights. Always giggling. Always grabbing at her, pawing her.

She just hadn't been able to get Bill out of her mind.

She turned to Eric. His eyes were focused straight ahead on the road. Caught in the glare of the headlights, the snow seemed to be swirling in every direction now.

"Don't be mad at me," Becka said softly.

"I'm not," Eric told her. He shrugged.

The shrug, so casual, so cool, made her angry.

I guess he wanted to break up too, she thought. I guess he's glad.

It wasn't what she had expected.

She hadn't expected that shrug. As if all the weeks they'd been going together were nothing.

Something to shrug off in a second.

Now she was angry. And upset.

Why do I always have to take things more seriously than everyone else? she wondered.

By the time he turned onto Fear Street and pulled up her driveway, she was trembling. She pushed open her door. A blast of cold air invaded the car at once.

"See you in school," Eric said brightly. "It's been real."

So cruel, Becka thought miserably.

He didn't care about me at all.

She slammed the car door behind her. He didn't wait for her to go into her house. He backed down the drive and was gone while she still stood searching her jeans pocket for her keys.

Her thoughts swirled in crazy directions, like the falling snow.

I can't go inside yet. I'm too upset.

She had the keys to her parents' car with her house key.

I'll go see Bill.

No, I'll just drive for a bit. Try to calm myself down.

She headed for the garage, her boots crunching the fresh snow. She slowly pulled the overhead door up, raising it as quietly as she could so her parents wouldn't hear.

A few seconds later she backed out of the drive, the headlights off, then roared off down Fear Street, the tires skidding beneath her.

The snow is so pretty, she thought, clicking on the headlights, leaning forward to peer out the windshield. I'll just drive around town, then come back.

Her heart was still racing. Her stomach felt as if it had been tied in knots.

I was so nervous about breaking up with Eric, she thought, turning onto the Mill Road. And now that I've done it, I'm even more nervous.

It doesn't make sense.

But that's just the way I am, Becka realized. I always feel more nervous after something happens.

Face it, kid, she told herself, you're nervous. Period.

I've got to call Bill, she thought. I've got to call Trish and Lilah too.

They'll be surprised that I broke up with Eric.

More surprised than Eric, she thought unhappily.

She pictured his shrug again. The blank, uncaring look on his face.

Who *needs* him? she thought.

Lost in her thoughts, she didn't see the four-way stop in time.

When the side of the red Corsica appeared just ahead of her in the windshield, it was too late.

Becka gasped and hit the brakes. Her car slid hard into the other car.

She closed her eyes against the crunch of metal and shattering glass.

chapter

2

"I can't believe you didn't get a scratch!" Trish exclaimed.

"I wasn't going that fast," Becka replied. "Because of the snow. Our car wasn't even that badly messed up. Just one headlight got smashed."

"You were so lucky," Lilah said.

"Well . . . I wouldn't exactly call it lucky," Becka told them. "My dad really yelled at me for taking the car without permission."

Trish and Lilah tsk-tsked.

It was the next afternoon, a bright, blue-skied Saturday, the ground covered with snow, still fresh and white. Becka and her two friends were upstairs in Becka's room, warm and comfortable, the old radiator against the wall making hissing sounds.

Becka, dressed in black yoga pants and an over-size blue wool pullover, sat on her bed, back pressed against the wall, legs crossed. She was knitting furiously, a ball of olive green yarn in her lap. "I'll never get this sweater finished by Christmas," she muttered.

"Becka, who's it a present for?" Lilah asked, raising her head from the shaggy white carpet where she lay on her stomach, flipping through an old copy of *Teen*.

"My cousin. Ow!" Becka cried. "I poked myself." She held up her finger to examine the small, bright red circle of blood. "Now I'm going to drip on the sweater."

She tossed the knitting down and scrambled over to her dresser to get a tissue.

"I knit to calm me down, but it doesn't seem to be working today," Becka told them, pressing the tissue against the cut. "Every Christmas my cousin Rachel and I knit sweaters for each other. Hers is always perfect, with these perfect little stitches, and perfect little patterns, and mine . . ." Her voice trailed off.

"Take it easy," Lilah said, closing the magazine and rolling onto her back, her hands under her head. Lilah wore a maroon-and-white Shadyside High sweatshirt over faded jeans, ripped at both knees.

"You need a Band-Aid," Trish said from the window seat across the room. She had been staring out at the snow-covered front yard, but turned to check out Becka's injury.

"How can I knit with a Band-Aid on my finger?" Becka snapped.

"Badly?" Trish joked. Her blue eyes lit up. She grinned, exposing her braces, braces she had worn for a year but still made her self-conscious. Dressed in gray sweats, Trish was short and chubby with curly auburn hair that capped her lively, mischievous face.

"Love the haircut," Lilah called up from her place on the carpet.

9

"Yeah. It's awesome," Trish added enthusiastically.

Becka peered at her reflection in the dresser mirror. "It's too short," she said uncertainly.

"No way," Trish declared.

Becka had seen the ultra-short haircut on a model in *Seventeen*. The model looked a lot like Becka. Light blond hair, almond-shaped green eyes, high cheekbones, pale white skin, and just the hint of a cleft in her chin. So Becka had taken a chance and had almost all her hair cut off, emerging with a sleek, chic new look.

"I look like a boy," Becka insisted.

"You look great," Trish told her.

"Stop fishing for compliments," Lilah said, rolling her eyes. "You look great and you *know* you do."

"I'm so jealous," Trish said from the window seat. "With my round face, I could never wear my hair short like that. I'd look like a bowling ball with legs!"

"I'd rather look like a bowling ball than a stork!" Lilah grumbled. She secretly liked being tall, but constantly complained about it.

Becka removed the tissue from her finger. "There. I think it's stopped bleeding." She stepped over Lilah on her way back to the bed and picked up her knitting. "Like this color?" she asked Lilah.

"Yeah. It's great. Your cousin's color blind, right?" Trish laughed.

"Don't encourage her," Becka said to Trish, frowning. "Hey, you know, my neck *is* a little stiff. From the accident, I guess."

"What a night you had," Trish said, shaking her head. "First you wreck Eric. Then you wreck the car."

Lilah laughed. "You should be a writer, Trish. You have such a way with words."

THE BEST FRIEND

"Eric wasn't too wrecked," Becka said dryly, trying to remember where she was in the pattern.

"Give us more details," Trish demanded, walking over and sitting on the edge of the bed. "We want more details."

"I already told you everything," Becka said. "I broke up with Eric. I told him I thought we shouldn't go out anymore. And he sat there like a lump. He barely said a word. He acted so cold, the coldest thing I ever saw."

"He didn't burst into tears and beg for one more chance through pitiful sobs?" Trish asked.

Lilah laughed. "I can just picture that. Poor Eric."

"No. No tears. No nothing. He just shrugged," Becka said. "Really. It was so obnoxious."

"He was speechless, that's all," Lilah offered. "He was in shock."

"Yeah. Sure," Becka said sarcastically. "Does this look long enough to you?" She held up the knitting.

"Long enough for what?" Trish asked. "For a scarf?"

"It's a sleeve," Becka told her.

"Is it one sleeve or two?" Trish demanded.

"Huh? It's one."

"It's long enough," Trish said.

All three girls laughed.

Becka was starting to relax, to feel a little calmer.

"Did you tell Eric about Bill?" Lilah demanded, performing some slow sit-ups on the carpet, her hands still behind her head.

"No. Of course not," Becka replied.

"That would've gotten a reaction from him!" Trish declared.

"Sshhh!" Becka held a finger to her lips. "It would

get a big reaction from my mom, too. Careful. I think she's up here, cleaning the guest room."

Trish and Lilah peered out the doorway. Trish got up and closed the door.

"Now she'll know we're up to something," Becka said, her brow furrowed as she counted stitches.

"What has your mom got against Bill, anyway?" Lilah asked, whispering even though the door was now closed.

"Oh, you know," Becka replied, frowning. "That trouble he got into at school last year."

"But that wasn't his fault," Lilah said, jumping to Bill's defense. "It was those two creeps, Mickey Wakely and Clay Parker. They admitted they were the ones who broke into the school and spray-painted all that stuff."

"But Bill was with them," Becka said. "He didn't do anything, but he was there."

"Wrong place, wrong time," Trish said, shaking her head.

"But Mickey and Clay—" Lilah started.

"Bill was suspended too, remember?" Becka interrupted. "Well, my parents remember it. Too well. After Bill was suspended, that was it. I wasn't allowed to see him or call him or anything."

"I remember," Trish said sympathetically. "You nearly freaked."

"We thought you were sick or something," Lilah added, continuing her sit-ups. "You were really messed up."

"Yeah," Becka recalled unhappily. Her green eyes lit up. "But that was last year. This year it will be different, I think. I hope. I mean, Bill has really straightened himself out. He isn't hanging out with

Mickey and Clay anymore. He's got a really good attitude, and—"

Before Becka could finish her sentence, the bedroom door was flung open. Becka dropped her knitting. Lilah sat up straight. Trish leapt to her feet.

All three of them stared in surprise as a girl with a mane of long auburn hair excitedly swept into the room. "Hi!" she shouted, her eyes darting from girl to girl, finally landing on Becka.

"Becka!" the girl cried. Stepping over Lilah, she bent down, threw her arms around Becka, and wrapped her up in a tight hug. "Becka! Becka! I'm so happy to see you!" she squealed.

Her mouth open wide in bewilderment, Becka struggled unsuccessfully to free herself from the girl's hug.

"I can't believe it!" the girl cried. "I just can't believe it! Becka, it's you! It's really *you!*"

Becka gasped, utterly speechless. Who *is* this girl? she asked herself.

I've never seen her before!

chapter
3

"I just can't believe it!" the girl cried, finally letting go of Becka and taking a step back. She tugged at her thick auburn hair, tossing it back over her shoulder as she shrugged out of her coat. "I just can't believe I'm here!"

Becka scrambled off the bed and nearly tripped over Lilah, who was climbing to her feet, confusion on her face.

Do I *know* her? Becka asked herself, staring hard at the intruder, studying her face, struggling to call up some memory of her.

Have I ever seen her before?

She was about Becka's size, but with a full figure.

She wasn't exactly pretty. But she was very dramatic looking with her flowing auburn hair down past her shoulders, round, gray eyes, and full lips coated in dark lipstick. She wore a bright orange sweater that clashed with her hair and a green miniskirt over black tights.

Becka couldn't help but notice the girl's hands, which were balled into tight fists at her sides. They were so big. They seemed to be the wrong size, out of proportion for the rest of her.

"The door was open downstairs, so I let myself in. Do you believe I moved right next door?" the girl gushed. "Isn't that the most *amazing* coincidence?"

Who is she? Becka wondered, frantically searching her memory. She saw tears form in the corners of the girl's big gray eyes.

She's so emotional, Becka thought. So excited to see me. So overjoyed. I must know her. I *must*.

She turned to Trish for help. But Trish only returned her glance with a wide-eyed shrug. Lilah was staring at the girl too, bewilderment on her face.

"Oh, Becka, you look exactly the same!" the girl cried and stepped forward to wrap Becka in another emotional hug.

"So do you," Becka managed to reply, staring over the girl's shoulder at Lilah, motioning for Lilah to help her.

"Hi, I'm Lilah Brewer," Lilah said when the girl had once again let go of Becka. "I don't think we've met. And this is Trish. Trish Walters," Lilah said, pointing to Trish who had backed up to the window seat.

"Hi." Trish gave the girl an awkward smile. Her silver braces gleamed in the light from the window.

The girl turned away from Becka, a startled expression on her face, as if she hadn't realized there were other people in the room. "I remember you two," she said, wiping the tears from her eyes with her big hands. "I'm Honey Perkins."

Who? Becka wondered, staring hard at the girl.

Do I know a Honey Perkins?

Is this some kind of a mistake or something?

Honey turned back to Becka, her smile growing wider. "I can't believe it. I just can't. Do you believe we're moving in next door? Isn't that amazing?"

"Yeah," Becka said, trying to work up some enthusiasm. "It's amazing!"

"Wow!" Honey exclaimed, staring hard at Becka. "Wow! I'm sorry, but I'm just speechless."

"Me too," Becka replied.

Why can't I remember her? Am I losing my mind?

"Are you going to Shadyside High?" Trish asked from in front of the window.

"Wow," Honey said, staring at Becka.

Does she have to stare at me like that? Becka thought uncomfortably. It's like I'm a hot fudge sundae she's about to devour!

"Did you used to go to our school, Honey?" Lilah asked.

Honey, her attention glued to Becka, didn't seem to hear the questions of the other two girls. "It's really you," she said to Becka.

"Yeah. It's me all right," Becka replied.

I can't take much more of this, Becka thought. Who *is* she and what does she *want?*

Wiping more tears from her eyes, Honey finally turned to Lilah and Trish. "Sorry I'm so emotional," she said, shaking her head. "But Becka and I— You see, we were best best friends in third and fourth grade. And I just can't believe I'm back!"

She lunged forward and wrapped Becka in another hug.

Best best friends? Becka thought.

I don't remember having a best friend named Honey.

My best friend in fourth grade was Deena Martinson.

Grinning at Becka, Honey pushed her thick hair up high on her head with both hands. "This is awesome. It's just awesome!"

Becka sank back onto the edge of her bed. "It sure is." She motioned for Honey to take the chair in front of her dressing table.

"I'm so excited, I don't know if I can sit down," Honey said. But she quickly pulled the chair in front of Becka and sat down, crossing her legs, tapping one sneaker on the carpet.

"So where did you move after fourth grade?" Lilah asked, dropping down to the floor, leaning back against Becka's bed and tucking her long legs under her.

Honey didn't seem to hear Lilah. She stared at Becka. "When I heard we were moving to Fear Street, my first thought was, Does Becka still live there? And sure enough, you do. In the very same house."

"Yeah. My parents love this old house," Becka said, glancing across the room at Trish.

"That's so great! We're next-door neighbors now!" Honey gushed.

"Where have you been living?" Trish asked.

"It's just my dad and me," Honey told Becka. "Mom died last year. It's been tough, very hard on both of us. Very hard."

Is Honey ignoring Trish and Lilah? Becka wondered. Doesn't she hear their questions?

Honey had pulled the chair right up in front of

Becka, as if the other two girls weren't part of the conversation.

"That's one reason I'm so happy you're still here," Honey continued, beaming at Becka, her enormous gray eyes burning into Becka's. "So it'll be a lot like old times. I mean, so we can be best friends again."

To her surprise, Becka suddenly found herself feeling guilty. She obviously had been important in Honey's life. Their friendship obviously meant a lot to Honey. But Becka couldn't even remember knowing Honey.

Some friend I am, Becka thought, scolding herself. What's *wrong* with me, anyway?

Trish said something from the window seat. Honey ignored her again. "You've got to tell me all about yourself," she told Becka. "We've got so much catching up to do."

"There isn't much to tell," Becka replied uncomfortably.

Suddenly Becka's mother poked her head into the bedroom. "How's it going in here?" she asked, her eyes moving from face to face.

"Mrs. Norwood!" Honey shrieked, excitedly leaping up from her chair. She dove across the room and wrapped Becka's mom in an emotional hug.

Mrs. Norwood cast an astonished glance at Becka.

"It's so good to see you again! You look *wonderful!*" Honey cried.

"Well, thanks," Becka's mom sputtered. "So do you, dear."

"I moved in right next door!" Honey exclaimed, her arm still around Mrs. Norwood's slender waist. "Isn't that amazing?"

18

"Yes. I guess it is," Becka's mom replied uncertainly. "That's really nice." She made an excuse and quickly retreated from the room.

Honey turned back to Becka. "Your mom is so great. I always thought she was really neat."

"Yeah. She's okay," Becka replied.

Mom didn't recognize Honey either, Becka realized. That made Becka feel a little better, a little less guilty.

But not much.

"She looks a lot older," Honey said, her smile fading. "She shouldn't let her hair go gray. She should color it."

"She does color it," Becka replied. "She's been really busy lately, so—"

"I'd like to color my hair," Lilah said, running a hand through her brown ponytail. "Brown is such a blah color. But my mom said she'd kill me if I did anything to it."

"At least *your* hair is straight," Trish complained.

"Oh. I love that pin. What's that pin?" Honey asked, ignoring Trish and Lilah and picking up a pin from Becka's dresser top.

"It's a parrot," Becka told her, stepping up beside her. "Bill—uh—my old boyfriend, gave it to me because I like birds."

"You always loved animals," Honey said, holding the pin up to admire it. "Remember that injured bird we found? You took it home and tried to nurse it back to health? Remember how we cried and cried when the little bird died?"

No, thought Becka. I don't remember.

"Yeah," she told Honey. "I remember."

19

"Can I try it on?" Honey asked, holding it up to her orange sweater. "Is it plastic?"

"No. It's enamel," Becka told her.

"You were always so stylish," Honey said, standing in front of the mirror with the pin. "You always knew the latest thing to wear. You always looked so great. I *love* your haircut. It's just so perfect for you."

"Thanks," Becka said, glancing at Trish, who was staring out the window.

Honey admired the parrot pin in the mirror, a pleased smile on her face.

"I think it's going to snow again," Trish said. "Look how dark it's getting."

"It better not," Lilah said, standing up and stretching. "We're supposed to drive to my cousin's tonight. The roads are already so slippery."

"I'll bet we have a white Christmas this year," Trish said.

"My sweater. I'll never get it finished in time!" Becka complained.

"Why don't you buy one and say that you knitted it?" Lilah suggested.

"It would be too good," Becka replied.

"Buy a bad one!" Lilah said.

Becka and Trish laughed.

Honey didn't seem to hear the conversation. "I love your room," she said, her eyes studying the posters above Becka's bed. "It's small, but you've got everything you need. You just have such good taste."

"Thanks," Becka replied awkwardly.

"I want my room to be just like this," Honey said thoughtfully. "I even want the same posters."

"I'm kind of tired of them," Becka told her.

"Really? Can I have them?" Honey asked. "I mean, if you don't want them anymore?"

Becka wasn't really ready to pull them down. She had just been making conversation. But now Honey was staring at her intently, eagerly waiting for an answer.

"Yeah. I guess," she said with a shrug.

"Great! You don't have to take them down now. I'm still unpacking cartons in my room," Honey told her. "Anyway. I can get them some other time. I'll be seeing you a lot."

Becka didn't reply. She glanced reluctantly at her posters.

I don't really want to give them away, she realized. I should've told Honey no.

Why did I offer to give them to her?

Honey glanced at the clock on Becka's dresser. "Wow. I've got to get going." She turned back to Becka, her face revealing deep emotion. "Oh, I hope we can be best friends again!" she cried. "Just like when we were kids."

She rushed forward and gave Becka another hug. Then she turned and ran out of the room.

Becka, Lilah, and Trish remained silent, listening to Honey's heavy footsteps descend the stairs. When they heard the front door slam, all three of them exploded at once.

"What was *that* all about?" Trish demanded.

"She didn't even notice Trish and I were here!" Lilah exclaimed. "She didn't say goodbye or anything!"

"Who is she?" Becka asked, collapsing onto the floor beside Lilah. "Am I cracking up or what?"

"She's your best friend, Becka," Lilah said in a mock scolding tone. "How could you forget your best friend?"

Laughing, Trish buried her face in a window seat pillow.

"Do you remember her?" Becka demanded.

Lilah and Trish shook their heads.

"Why should *we* remember her?" Trish said. "She was *your* best best best best best friend!"

Trish and Lilah collapsed in hysterics.

Becka didn't join in. She pulled the pillow out of Trish's hands and hugged it. "But—but what if she was right? What if we *were* best best friends? How could I be so awful to forget?"

"Face it. You're awful!" Trish declared. She and Lilah both thought this remark was hilarious too.

Becka heaved the pillow at Trish. It missed and bounced off the window.

"You'll probably forget us too," Lilah declared.

"Forget who?" Trish cried.

Both she and Lilah collapsed in laughter.

"Come on," Becka urged. "This is serious. Did you see how happy Honey was to see me? And all I could do was stand there with my mouth open and go, 'Duhhh.'"

"I've never seen her before," Trish said. "Weren't we in the same fourth grade class? Didn't you have Miss Martin?"

"Yeah," Becka said.

"Me too," said Lilah. "Whatever happened to Miss Martin?"

"Moved away, I think," Becka replied. "I think she had a baby and got married."

"Don't you mean got married and had a baby?" asked Lilah.

"Whatever," Becka replied impatiently.

"So why don't we remember Honey Perkins?" Lilah asked.

"Do you have your class pictures?" Trish demanded, standing up and walking over to the other two.

"From fourth grade?" Becka shook her head. "I don't think so. Oh. Wait." She made her way to the desk against the wall, leaned down, and pulled out the bottom drawer. "I might have it in this box."

She pulled out a battered cardboard box and began rummaging through it. A short while later she lifted out their fourth grade class picture.

The girls huddled close to study it.

"There she is," Trish said, putting her finger on a face in the upper right-hand corner. "It's got to be her. The same hair."

And as Trish pulled her finger away, all three girls suddenly remembered Honey.

"Yeah. Right. That's her," Becka recalled. "She was weird."

"She was real weird," Trish agreed. "She was quiet. Almost never spoke. When Miss Martin called on her, she used to choke. Remember? She'd turn real white and just sputter."

"No one liked her," Lilah commented, staring hard at the photo. "Hey, Becka, nice bangs!" she cried, pointing to Becka in the front row.

"You were always so stylish!" Trish teased.

Becka gave her a hard poke in the ribs and returned to staring at Honey's unsmiling face. "Honey used to

23

burst into loud sobs for no reason at all," she remembered.

"Yeah. She was scary," Trish added.

"She had no friends at all," Lilah said.

"So why does she think that she and I were such good pals?" Becka asked.

"She must have an *awesome* fantasy life," Trish mused.

"Guess you're real lucky to have a new admirer," Lilah teased Becka.

"Yeah. A new best best friend," Trish said, grinning.

Becka frowned. "I'm not so sure."

She put the photo back in the box and replaced the box in the desk drawer. They talked about Honey for a little while longer, remembering what a strange, lonely girl she had been.

"She moved away before the end of fourth grade," Lilah recalled. "I remember now. She sat next to me. And then one day her desk was empty."

"I've got to go," Trish said abruptly. "Talk to you later, Becka. It's been real."

She started toward the door, Lilah following. "Wait up. I'll walk with you. Call you later," she told Becka.

Becka didn't seem to hear their farewells. "Hey—my pin," she said.

Lilah and Trish turned back to see Becka gaping at her dresser top. "Huh?"

"My parrot pin," Becka exclaimed. "It's gone!"

chapter
4

"*D*id Honey take it?" Lilah asked.

"I thought I saw her put it back on the dresser," Trish said.

"Well, it's not there now," Becka muttered unhappily. She was down on her hands and knees, searching the carpet around the dresser.

Lilah and Trish quickly joined in the search. "It's not on the desk," Trish reported.

"Look under the desk. Maybe it fell," Lilah suggested.

"I love that pin," Becka said, bending low to peer under the dresser. "It's the only present Bill ever gave me, and it's my absolute favorite."

"And it's so stylish. Don't forget stylish," Trish joked, mocking Honey.

"Very funny," Becka said under her breath. She climbed to her feet. "She stole it! Honey stole my pin!" she cried, hands on her hips.

"She didn't *steal* it," Trish said, still searching, her

head under the bed. "She probably forgot she had it on."

"Yeah. I'm sure she didn't deliberately take it," Lilah agreed.

"If I've lost that pin, I'll be so upset," Becka said heatedly, searching the top of the dresser again.

"Go ask Honey for it," Trish suggested, climbing to her feet, brushing herself off. "It's probably still on her sweater."

"That tacky orange sweater," Lilah commented, making a face.

"What was wrong with her sweater? I liked it," Trish replied.

"Honey looked like a pumpkin in it," Becka said absently, concentrating on her search.

"You redheads stick together," Lilah accused Trish. "Maybe *you* should be Honey's best friend."

"I'm going next door to get my pin back," Becka said. "You two coming with me?"

"What for?" Trish asked.

"I'm going home," Lilah said, glancing at her watch. "Talk to you later."

Trish and Lilah disappeared down the stairs. Becka continued her search for a little while longer. But the pin definitely was not in the room.

Glancing out the window, Becka saw that it had started to snow again. Big flakes drifted down slowly, rocking from side to side like white feathers as they fell.

I'll run next door to ask Honey for my pin, Becka decided. She pulled her parka from the closet, and was slipping into it when the phone rang.

She made a dive for the phone extension on her desk, but she wasn't quick enough. It stopped after the first ring. Her mother must have answered it downstairs.

Leaning against the desk, Becka waited with the parka on to see if the call was for her. Sure enough, a few seconds later, her mother called up from the bottom of the stairs.

"Becka, phone for you." Mrs. Norwood's voice revealed her disapproval. "It's Bill. Why is he calling you, Becka? You know you're not allowed to see him."

"I know, Mom," Becka shouted down angrily. "Spare me the lectures, okay?"

She picked up the phone, listened for her mother's retreating footsteps, then said hello to Bill.

"Bill, hi. How's it going?"

"Hi, Becka. I'm okay." He sounded far away. There was a lot of interference. He must be calling from a pay phone, Becka decided. "Your mom didn't sound too friendly," he said.

"She was just surprised to hear you," Becka lied.

"She never liked me much. I think it's my pierced ear."

"She's used to that," Becka told him. "Why are we talking about my mother?"

He chuckled. "Beats me." She loved his voice. It was soft and smooth. Musical. "Hey, can you meet me tonight?"

"Where?" Becka realized she was whispering even though her mother was nowhere near.

"Meet me at the mall?"

"I don't think so," Becka replied, hesitantly, thinking hard.

"How come? Because of your mom?"

"And my dad," Becka joked. "Don't forget my dad. He doesn't like you either."

"So does that mean you'll meet me?" Bill asked slyly.

She loved his sense of humor. Even when things were going wrong for him and he found himself suspended from school and in deep trouble, he had still been able to make jokes about it.

"No. I'd better not," Becka whispered. "I'd like to, but . . ."

"Is that a yes?"

"No. I mean—"

"Sneak out," he urged. "Wait till they're asleep, and sneak out."

"Bill, you know my parents stay up really late," Becka replied, shaking her head. Suddenly she had an unpleasant thought. "Mom, are you listening in on the extension?" she asked loudly.

She listened for the click of the downstairs phone being hung up, but there was none.

"Whew."

"I thought you were going to talk to your parents," Bill said, sounding hurt. "You know. Tell them what a good guy I am now."

"I'm going to," Becka said, feeling guilty. "It just hasn't been the right time." And then she quickly added, "I'm sure they'll understand. I'm sure they'll give you another chance, Bill."

"Yeah. Sure," he muttered bitterly. "Are you going to sneak out and meet me tonight or not, Becka?"

Becka hesitated. "I don't think so. Not tonight," she decided.

"That's okay. I'm busy anyway," Bill joked.

She laughed. "Very funny."

"I am very funny," he insisted.

"Yeah, funny looking."

"Is that *your* idea of a joke?"

Becka heard her mother approaching the stairs. "I've got to go. Bye, Bill. See you." She hung up quickly.

She was halfway down the stairs, the heavy parka sailing out behind her, when her mother appeared in the hall. "What did Bill want?" she asked, frowning.

"Just wanted to say hi," Becka replied, stopping a few steps before the floor.

"You know how your dad and I feel about him, Becka."

"Yeah. I know. But Bill is different now, Mom. He—"

"Especially after what happened to you, what you went through afterward." Mrs. Norwood got that faraway look in her pale blue eyes, the look she always got when she was recalling something bad that had happened. "You were so hurt. So upset. Your father and I don't want to see you that upset again."

"Mom—" Becka started, but restrained herself.

"Where are you going? It's almost dinnertime," her mother said, noticing the parka.

"I'm not sneaking out to meet, Bill, if that's what you mean," Becka replied shrilly.

"Becka—!"

"I'm just going next door. I'll be right back." Becka pushed past her mother and out the front door. She slammed the door behind her and stepped out into the snow.

She raised her face to the sky. The cold snowflakes felt good on her hot cheeks.

Sometimes her mother made her *so mad*. What business was it of hers if Becka wanted to go out with Bill?

"When is she going to stop interfering in my life?" Becka cried aloud. "When?" she demanded of the sky.

She got a snowflake on her tongue in reply.

She lowered her head, pulling the parka hood over her hair, and began to trudge across her snow-covered front yard to Honey's house.

The house had been vacant for several months. Becka eased her way through the untrimmed hedge that divided the two yards. The tall weeds that had taken over the unmowed lawn poked up through the snow.

It'll be good to have someone in the house, she thought. It was so creepy to see it standing empty like that.

Approaching the front of the house, she stopped just past the snow-covered driveway.

And looked up at the house—and gasped.

chapter

5

*T*he house is still empty, Becka realized with a shudder.

Honey had lied about moving next door.

A gust of wind sent a curtain of powdery snow across the yard. The bare trees rattled and creaked, then resumed their silent watch over the house.

The dark, still house.

Becka stared from window to window, searching for a light, any sign of life. But the old house, snow drifts pushed up against its dark shingles, icicles hanging from the low roof of the front stoop, appeared as empty and deserted as it had for months.

"How can this be?" Becka said aloud.

As she trudged up the unshoveled walk to the ice-covered front steps, she felt a shiver run down her back, a shiver of dread.

There were footprints in the snow, but they were old, half filled in by the afternoon's snowfall.

Becka slipped on the first step, but stopped herself

from falling by grabbing onto the metal rain downspout beside the stoop. Making her way more carefully, she crossed the small, square stoop and pounded hard on the front door.

Silence.

Leaning off the stoop, she peeked into the living room window.

Darkness inside.

Were those cartons against the wall? Too dark to tell.

She knocked again. Tried the doorbell, but the button was frozen in place.

Silence.

Another wind gust tossed a swirl of powdery snow onto the stoop.

Shivering, Becka turned away from the dark, empty house, carefully made her way down the frozen stairs, and started to jog home.

Where is Honey? she wondered, questions swirling across her mind like the flakes of snow being tossed by the wind. *Why did she appear so suddenly and lie about moving in next door? Where is my parrot pin? There's* got *to be a logical explanation for this—right?*

Right?

"Did you see Mary Harwood when she came out of the supply closet with David Metcalf? She had a big purple spot on her neck." Lilah shook her head and giggled.

Becka stopped walking and gaped at her friend. "You mean a hickey?"

Lilah rolled her eyes. "Mary said it was a mosquito bite. Isn't that lame? A mosquito bite in December?"

Both girls laughed and began walking again. It was a bright afternoon, the sun high in the sky, making the melting snow sparkle like silver. School had just let out, and they had decided to walk home.

"What's with Mary's mother?" Becka asked, shifting her backpack from one shoulder to the other, then adjusting the hood of her parka. "Doesn't she know what a tramp Mary is?"

"She has no idea," Lilah replied, an amused grin on her face. "Mary's mom lives on some other planet. Billy Harper told Lisa Blume that he was making out with Mary Saturday afternoon on the couch in Mary's living room. Mary's mom walked up to them with a tray and asked if anyone wanted homemade fudge!"

This story made them both laugh gleefully.

"Wow!" Becka exclaimed. "And my mom monitors every phone call I get!"

"Speaking of phone calls," said Lilah, turning serious, "did you hear from Bill again?"

Becka shook her head. "No. He's probably angry with me because I wouldn't sneak out and meet him at the mall Saturday night."

They crossed the street. Becka had to hurry to keep up with Lilah's long strides.

The blare of a car horn startled them both. They turned to see a station wagon rumble by, filled with kids they knew from school. It stopped in the middle of the intersection. The driver's window rolled down, and Ricky Schorr poked his grinning head out.

"Want a ride?"

"There's no room," Becka told him, pointing to the crowd jammed into the back of the wagon.

"You can sit on my lap!" Ricky yelled.

The car exploded with raucous laughter.

"I'd rather walk home barefoot," Becka shot back. She and Lilah turned and continued on their way. The station wagon rumbled on.

"Ricky's friends think he's a riot," Becka muttered.

"Since when does he have friends?"

"Since he began driving that station wagon to school," Becka replied.

"So did you tell your parents you want to start seeing Bill again?"

Becka shook her head. "I haven't been in the mood for World War Three."

"Are you going to sneak out and see him?"

"No. Maybe. I don't know. I can't decide."

"You sound pretty undecided," Lilah said. She stopped to wave to a man and a woman in the yard across the street. The man was up on a ladder, stringing a row of Christmas lights along his roof edge. His wife was on the ground, helping to untangle them.

"The Andersons really get into Christmas," Lilah said softly. "Look at all those lights. Their house looks like one of those Las Vegas casinos! Can you imagine their electric bill?"

"Well, at least I'll get to see Bill at Trish's Christmas party," Becka said, sighing.

"He's coming?"

"Yeah. Who isn't? It's going to be a mob scene. Trish has invited everyone in the world!"

"Did you buy a dress?" Lilah asked, kicking a clump of hardened snow along the walk.

"I got a great skirt," Becka said enthusiastically. "It's really short and really silky. It's silver. I'm going to wear it over that black catsuit I bought at the mall."

"I can't wear a catsuit. I look like a broom," Lilah complained.

"I can't believe you're unhappy about being tall," Becka told her. "I would *kill* to be as tall as you."

"No, you wouldn't."

"Well . . . *almost* as tall as you!"

Both girls laughed. They said their goodbyes, promising to call each other later. Becka watched Lilah jog over the snow toward her house, her long brown ponytail bobbing out from under her blue wool cap. Then Becka turned and headed for Fear Street, thinking about Bill and about Trish's party.

"Anyone home?" she called, stepping inside the kitchen and closing the door behind her. The kitchen was warm and smelled of cinnamon. There was no reply.

Becka made her way through the back hall and started up the stairs to her room to get rid of her backpack. She stopped halfway up and listened.

A voice upstairs.

A voice from her room.

Was it her mother? Who was she talking to?

Becka climbed two more stairs and stopped. Hidden by the railing, she peered across the landing into her room.

The door was open more than halfway. The lights were on. Becka could see a portion of her bed.

Someone was moving around in there, chatting.

Someone.

Becka poked her face through the railing and watched.

Honey!

Staring across the dark hallway, Becka saw Honey deposit some clothes on Becka's bed.

My clothes, Becka realized. What is going on here?

Honey is in my room, taking clothes out of my closet.

Honey disappeared from view. Becka heard her voice but couldn't make out what she was saying.

When she reappeared, Becka recognized the skirt Honey was wearing. It was the silver skirt Becka had bought for Trish's party.

She's wearing my skirt?

Becka gripped the rail tightly, frozen, staring in disbelief at what the rectangle of light revealed in the doorway to her bedroom.

She's wearing my skirt!

She was also wearing a silky blue top that Becka's parents had given her for her birthday.

Once again, Honey stepped out of view. Becka could hear her opening dresser drawers now.

What is she doing here?

Why is she in my room, trying on my best clothes?

And who, Becka wondered, *is Honey talking to?*

chapter

6

"*H*oney!" Becka burst in to her bedroom, her heart pounding.

"Oh, hi." Honey stood up from the dresser drawer she had been leaning over. A smile spread across her face. "You're home."

Becka gaped at her, speechless for a moment. Her eyes darted around the room. Honey, she saw, had removed most of the clothes from the closet and piled them on the bed.

"Uh—I didn't know—I mean, I didn't expect . . ." Becka stammered, feeling her face grow red.

"Your mom said I could come up," Honey said casually. She turned and pushed the dresser drawers closed.

"My mom? She's home?"

"No. I think she went out," Honey told her.

"Then who were you talking to?" Becka demanded, stepping reluctantly to the bed.

"Huh?" Honey stared at her, a bewildered expression on her face. She pushed back her disheveled pile of auburn hair.

"I heard you talking to someone," Becka insisted, turning to examine her nearly empty closet.

"No. Not me," Honey replied, her smile returning. "I'm all alone."

"But—" Becka realized she was still holding her backpack. She let it slide to the floor and kicked it under the bed.

"Oh, Becka, I just love your clothes!" Honey gushed. She swirled around in front of the mirror, admiring herself in the silver skirt and the silky blouse. "You always had such great taste! Even when we were little, you knew just what to buy."

"But, Honey—"

"I don't *believe* this skirt!" Honey exclaimed, not giving Becka a chance to get a word out. She spun around one more time, then walked over to Becka, stopping so close to her that Becka could smell the sweet chewing gum on her breath. Feeling awkward, Becka took a step back.

"I just bought that skirt. I haven't worn it yet," Becka said unhappily, hoping Honey would hear how irritated she was.

"Where did you get it?" Honey chirped. "Not at the mall. You couldn't have bought this skirt at one of those tacky shops at the mall. Where, Becka? You *have* to tell me! It's just so sexy!"

"At a little shop in the Old Village. Petermann's, I think," Becka muttered.

This can't be happening, Becka thought miserably.

Honey didn't seem to be picking up any of Becka's signals. She made her way back to the mirror to admire the outfit. "This top isn't exactly right. What else goes with the skirt?"

"I don't know," Becka said. "I'm going to wear the skirt to a Christmas party."

"Do you believe it?" Honey cried happily. "We're still the same size! I know I look bigger than you. But we're still the same size. We can still wear the same clothes, just like when we were kids."

"Really?" Becka uttered. She didn't know how to reply.

"People always said we looked like twins," Honey gushed, holding up a denim jumper and checking it out in the dresser mirror.

"They did?"

"We were always wearing each other's clothes. Always trading everything. Even our jeans. Even our socks. It was so amazing," Honey declared almost rapturously. "It got so we didn't know what was whose. We really were just like twins."

How come I don't remember that? Becka asked herself. It seems to me I'd remember that if it were true. Honey seems so sincere. I don't think she's deliberately lying.

Does she live in some kind of fantasy world?

"Do you like my hair up like this?" Honey asked, bunching her thick auburn hair with both hands and piling it in a bun on top of her head.

"Yeah. It's okay," Becka replied without enthusiasm.

"You're not looking!" Honey complained. "Look. Like this? Or, like this?" She let go of the hair and let it fall loosely behind her shoulders.

"It might be nice if you tied it loosely in back and

let it hang down," Becka suggested. "You know, with a wide ribbon."

"You're right!" Honey exclaimed happily. "You're always right about things like that! You're just amazing, Becka!" And she lunged across the room and gave Becka a long, heartfelt hug.

Becka gasped. She could barely breathe.

"I can't believe we're going to be best friends again!" Honey said, finally taking a step back. "I'm so happy, Becka. Aren't you?"

"Yeah." Becka tried to sound enthusiastic. But having gotten over her astonishment at finding Honey in her room, Becka remembered she had some important questions to ask.

"Honey, I went next door to see you Saturday afternoon," she said, searching Honey's face as if looking for answers. "But the house—it was totally dark and no one was there."

The smile faded slowly from Honey's face. She pushed back a strand of hair from her forehead. "I know. My dad couldn't get the furnace to start up. It was freezing in that old house. So we had to leave. Here I was so excited about moving into my new house, and Dad and I had to spend the weekend at a crummy motel."

"Oh, what a shame," Becka said, still studying Honey's face. "Is it okay now?"

"Yeah. The furnace guy finally came and we moved in," Honey said. "But I had to go to school today, so I still haven't had time to unpack."

Becka chewed her thumb nervously.

Do I believe her or not? she asked herself.

I guess I believe her.

THE BEST FRIEND

There was really no reason not to believe that story. It seemed perfectly logical.

"Do you have any ribbons?" Honey asked, fiddling with her hair. "I'd like to try tying it the way you suggested."

"I think I have some ribbons in my top drawer," Becka said. "But they might not be the right color." Becka took a deep breath. She realized she suddenly felt very nervous. "One more question."

"Uh-huh?"

Becka cleared her throat. "Know that parrot pin? The enamel one you tried on? Did you accidentally wear it home on Saturday?"

Honey hesitated for a brief moment.

Then, instead of answering, she reached out with both her large hands, grabbed Becka by the throat, and began to choke her.

chapter
7

Becka gaped as Honey's hands closed around her throat.

Struggling to twist out of Honey's tight grasp, Becka felt her breath catch.

She's strangling me!

I can't breathe!

Then, just as suddenly, the powerful hands let go.

Bending over, her hands pressed against her knees, Becka sucked in a deep lungful of air, let it out, and sucked in another.

When she looked up, Honey was laughing triumphantly.

"Gotcha!" Honey cried. "I gotcha that time!"

"You—" Becka tried to speak, but her throat was still choked and tight. "You *choked* me!" she managed to utter in a hoarse, strained voice.

Honey's laugh was cut short. "Hey—don't you remember our Gotcha game?"

"No. I—" Becka coughed. She was panting, her chest rising up and down, her heart still thudding.

"We used to do the *worst* things to each other," Honey recalled, shaking her head. "We always thought that Gotcha game was a riot. You remember —don't you, Becka?"

Becka didn't reply. Still breathing hard, she made her way to the mirror. Leaning close, she examined her neck. It was bright red, the skin rubbed raw.

"You *hurt* me!" Becka said angrily to Honey's reflection in the mirror.

Honey's smile faded quickly. Her dark lips formed a pout. "You forgot our Gotcha game?" she asked in a tiny voice, sounding hurt.

Becka tenderly rubbed her neck. She searched the cluttered dressing table until she found a bottle of skin lotion. Her back to Honey, she carefully rubbed the white lotion onto her scarlet neck.

"We used to shock each other all the time," Honey continued. "Remember that time in third grade when you pulled up my dress in front of that entire busload of Cub Scouts? That was the worst. The worst! I don't think I ever really paid you back for that one. Wow, that was funny! Fun times, huh, Becka?"

I don't remember any of that, Becka thought miserably. I really think she's making it all up. What's going on here?

"Listen, Honey," Becka said, leaning on the dressing table to stop her hands from trembling. "Did you accidentally take my parrot pin or not?"

"Sure, I took it," Honey replied without hesitating. "But it wasn't an accident."

Becka wheeled around in surprise. "Huh? What do you mean?"

Honey tossed a thick strand of hair behind her shoulders. "You gave it to me, Becka, remember?"

"Huh?" Becka's mouth dropped open in disbelief. "I *what?*"

"You gave the pin to me," Honey insisted cheerily.

"No I—"

"It was very sweet of you too," Honey said, a warm smile spreading across her face.

"No, Honey—wait," Becka said, feeling her pulse throb against her temples. "You asked to try the pin on, and—"

"And then you said that since I liked it so much, I could keep it." Honey's smile faded. She stared at Becka now with a hurt expression, her full lips lowered in another pout. "You did say I could keep it, Becka."

"But, Honey—" Becka suddenly realized that Honey was really upset. Her shoulders were trembling and her lips were quivering.

"Ask your friends," Honey said defensively. "Ask those two girls. They'll tell you. They saw you give it to me. Really."

Becka couldn't decide what to do. Honey, she saw, was about to burst into hysterical tears. Becka didn't want that. She wanted her pin back, but she didn't want a big emotional scene. Most of all, she just wanted Honey to leave.

"You gave the pin to me," Honey said, softening her tone, "and now it's my most special *special* possession. I will always treasure it, Becka."

"Well—uh, I'm glad you like it so much, Honey," Becka said weakly.

Honey was grinning now. No sign that she had been

about to cry or make an ugly scene. She plopped down on the bed, on top of one of Becka's best blouses.

"Uh—would you help me put this stuff back in the closet?" Becka asked, gathering up several pairs of jeans and slacks.

Then maybe I can get you to go home so I can call Bill, she thought.

"Oh. Sure." Honey popped up energetically. "I didn't get to try everything on. But there'll be plenty of time for that, right?"

"Yeah. Sure," Becka replied absently, shoving the jeans onto their shelf, then returning to the bed for more clothing.

Honey, meanwhile, was still standing by the side of the bed, making no move toward helping. "Oh, look! I got a stain on your top," she said, holding the stain up close. "What could that be?" she asked, consternation on her face. "I'd better go run some cold water on it."

"No, that's okay," Becka said quickly. "Just leave it. I've worn it before anyway. It has to go in the wash."

"No, really," Honey insisted. She stopped in the doorway. "Tell you what. I'll take it home and get the stain out. I'll wash it there and bring it back as good as new."

"No, really—" Becka started to say, but Honey had her mind made up.

As Becka returned her clothes to the closet, making several trips, Honey slipped out of the silver skirt and into her own faded jeans. "This is so exciting!" she exclaimed.

Becka, hanging the skirt in her closet, didn't respond.

"I hope you're not mad at me for getting the seating assignments changed in homeroom so we can sit together," Honey called to her. She was back sitting on the bed.

"No, no problem," Becka replied blankly.

"Just like the old days," Honey said happily. "You know, we can walk to school together every morning. Just like we used to."

"Sometimes my dad drives me," Becka told her, pushing the dresser drawers shut.

"Great!" Honey said. "That'll be great."

"And when the weather's nice, I sometimes ride my bike," Becka said. "It's good exercise."

"Yeah. I have to get a bike," Honey said thoughtfully. "You'll have to let me check out yours so I'll know what kind to get."

"Where did you move to when you left Shadyside?" Becka asked.

"Oh. Upstate," Honey answered vaguely. "What a drag that was. I didn't want to leave. Mainly, I didn't want to leave you, my best best friend. I can still remember that awful day so clearly, even though I was only nine. Can't you?"

"Yeah. I guess," Becka replied uncomfortably.

I don't even remember talking to her when I was nine!

"Remember the two of us, sitting on the curb in front of my house, our arms around each other's shoulders, crying and crying. Just crying our eyes out. Wow, that was awful. Remember?"

"Yeah," Becka said, avoiding Honey's stare.

"And remember that guy stopped his car and took our picture? He thought it was such a touching scene. He snapped our picture, and that made us cry even harder." Honey sighed and leaned back, supporting herself with her hands. "It was the worst day of my life, Becka. It really was."

"Well, I guess I'd better get downstairs now," Becka said awkwardly, turning her gaze to the bedroom door. "I haven't said hi to Mom, and—"

"I told you. She went out, I think," Honey said, not budging from the bed.

"Well, I've got some chores to do, and—"

"You want to come over and study tonight?" Honey asked. She glanced down and began rubbing at the stain on the silky blue top.

"Uh, I can't tonight," Becka told her.

"Well, how about tomorrow night?"

"Oh, I'm sorry, Honey. I can't tomorrow night, either," Becka said, telling the truth. "I promised Lilah I'd go over there and help her family decorate their tree."

"How nice," Honey said coldly, lowering her eyes. Then a strange, thoughtful look crossed her face, and she added, "You spend a lot of time with Lilah, don't you."

"Yeah. Lilah, Trish, and I are good buddies," Becka replied impatiently. "I have some chores to do and stuff, Honey, so . . ."

Honey pulled herself up from the bed. "Okay. What a nice visit." She grinned at Becka as she made her way across the room. "I feel as if I haven't been away a minute. Although, we have so much catching up to do. There's so much to talk about, so many things to share."

"Yeah," Becka replied awkwardly.

"See you first thing in the morning," Honey said, starting down the stairs. "I'll see myself out. Bye!"

Becka stood frozen in place with her eyes closed, not moving, not even breathing. She didn't move until she heard the front door slam shut behind Honey. Then she took a deep breath, let it out slowly, and walked out to the stairway.

"Mom, are you home? Mom?"

No reply.

Honey was right, Becka decided. Mom went out.

Good. I can talk to Bill without worrying. Without Mom butting in.

Becka hurried to her phone and punched in Bill's number. It rang twice before he picked it up.

"What are you doing?" Becka asked, whispering even though she was alone in the house.

He chuckled. "Would you believe *homework?*"

Bill should have graduated the previous spring. But because of his suspension and the fact that he had flunked most of his courses, this year was his second as a senior.

"This stuff makes a lot more sense the second time around," he said, only half joking. "I may even pass. What are you doing?"

Becka sighed. "That girl I told you about, Honey, my new neighbor, she came over. I mean, she was here when I got home."

"You don't sound too thrilled," Bill commented.

"Well . . . Honey comes on a little strong," Becka told him. "She's okay, I guess. She just makes me nervous."

"What *doesn't?*" Bill snickered.

"What's that supposed to mean?" Becka snapped.

"Nothing. Just kidding. I mean, you're not the *calmest* person in the world, Becka." He quickly changed the subject to get himself out of trouble. "Are you going to meet me Saturday night?"

Becka hesitated. "I don't know. I really don't want to sneak out."

"But, Becka—"

"I've always been honest with my parents, Bill. I'm not sure I want to start sneaking around behind their backs now."

"Then tell them you're meeting me," he urged.

"I want to. I just haven't found the right time. It seems—"

"I'm not a serial killer, you know," Bill said heatedly. "I got in a little trouble last year. But I'm totally straight now. I'm not going to corrupt the Norwoods' precious daughter." And then he added playfully, "Well . . . maybe a *little.*"

"I know, I know," Becka told him. "It's just that you don't know my parents."

"Well, I'd really like to see you Saturday night," Bill said curtly. "Maybe I'll come over and *really* freak them out."

Becka started to reply, but she heard her mother's car pull into the drive. "I've got to go. See you in school," she said breathlessly and hung up, her heart pounding.

She hurried downstairs to greet her mother.

Mrs. Norwood made her way through the kitchen door, carrying two bulging grocery bags. "It's so slushy out there," she complained, setting the bags down and bending to pull off her wet boots. "I hate it when the snow gets old and starts to melt."

She turned her attention to Becka. "How are you? What are you doing? Homework?"

49

"Not yet," Becka told her. "I've been busy with Honey."

"Honey?" Mrs. Norwood started to unpack the groceries.

"Yeah," Becka said, moving to the counter to help. "Why'd you let Honey go up to my room? You *know* I hate people trying on my stuff."

"Huh?" Becka's mom set down a bag of flour. "What are you talking about, Becka?"

"You didn't tell Honey it was okay for her to wait in my room?"

"How could I?" Mrs. Norwood asked, staring at Becka. "I haven't been home all afternoon."

chapter

8

"*T*hat was so much fun last night," Becka told Lilah. "I had a great time. Your little brother is a riot."

"You ever see anyone find so many ways to break tree ornaments?" Lilah asked, shaking her head.

"But the tree looked perfect," Becka said. "Scrawny but perfect."

It was Wednesday afternoon, a clear day, warm for winter, and only a few tiny patches of snow remained on the asphalt of the student parking lot. School had just let out. Becka and Lilah, backpacks slung on their shoulders, made their way toward the bike rack.

"Where do you want to ride?" Lilah asked, waving to some kids piling into a red Civic.

"Anywhere," Becka answered with enthusiasm. "I just want to ride and ride and ride. I feel as if I haven't used my legs in weeks."

"Yeah. Me too," Lilah replied. "I was so glad the snow finally melted so we could take our bikes. Let's take Park Drive to River Road, okay?"

Becka nodded. "The hills will be a challenge."

"It'll be really pretty up above the river," Lilah said. She stopped suddenly. "Look, there's your pal Honey at the bike rack."

Becka groaned. "Just my luck she moved in next door. She's like my shadow. Only closer."

"Why don't you tell her to get lost?" Lilah asked, stepping back as the red Civic roared past, its horn honking loudly.

"Sometimes I'd like to," Becka said thoughtfully. "But then I decide she's not so bad. I think she's just really insecure."

"Who isn't?" Lilah said dryly.

They made their way to the bike rack at the back of the student lot. Honey was examining one of the bikes, but she stepped away when she saw Becka and Lilah approaching. "Hi! How's it going?" she called, waving. She was wearing a yellow windbreaker. Her hair was tied behind her head with a yellow ribbon.

"Hiya, Honey," Lilah said cheerily.

Honey didn't seem to hear her. "Can I go home with you?" Honey asked Becka.

"No. Lilah and I are going for a long bike ride," Becka told her, tossing her backpack over the handlebars of her bike. "We've been sitting around for weeks. We need a workout."

Honey frowned. "I've got to get a bike. I want one just like yours. It's a ten-speed, right?"

Becka shook her head. "No. A twenty-one speed."

"I like your hair that way," Lilah said to Honey.

"Will you be home tonight?" Honey asked Becka.

"Yeah. I guess. I've got to work on my research paper for science."

"Me too," Honey said. "I'll call you, okay?"

"Okay," Becka said, backing her bike out of the rack.

"See you," Honey said. She stood beside the rack, her hands crammed in the pockets of her windbreaker, watching as Becka and Lilah pedaled away.

They made their way out of the parking lot and turned right onto Park Drive. The curb was still puddled with melting snow. Their tires sent up a spray as they rolled past.

"Did you see the look on Honey's face when you said she couldn't come with us?" Lilah called, pedaling hard a few yards ahead of Becka. "She looked as if you'd just killed her puppy."

"She's very emotional," Becka replied, leaning forward over her handlebars. "One minute she's ecstatically happy, the next she's ready to weep bitter tears."

"Weird," Lilah said.

They rode past the front of the school, the flag hanging limp on this windless afternoon, and headed through the neighborhood of big houses and tree-filled front yards known as North Hills.

"My legs ache already," Becka complained.

"We haven't even reached the good hills yet," Lilah said, pedaling harder.

"I've just been so lazy lately. This really feels good," Becka said.

"We're supposed to go skiing this vacation," Lilah

said, staring straight ahead as the road dipped to the east. "But we may not go. My dad may have to go to Akron on business."

"Akron? For Christmas?" Becka cried, pumping hard to keep up with her.

"No, he'd be back by Christmas. But we wouldn't be able to go away."

"What a drag," Becka groaned. She took her hands off the handlebars to unzip her jacket.

The sun was an orange ball just over the tops of the trees. In the center of a yard across the street lay a top hat and a straw broom, the remains of what must have been a pretty fancy snowman.

Becka pedaled rapidly to catch up to Lilah, and they biked side by side for a while. "Here come the hills," she warned.

"The first one is downhill. No problem!" Lilah cried.

"Watch out. There are still a few patches of ice," Becka said, pointing.

She stopped pedaling as they started to roll down the hill toward the intersection with River Road. The hill was steep, and they started to pick up speed.

Becka saw the brown delivery truck first. It was speeding toward the intersection, its engine roaring.

"Look out!" Becka warned. She pressed her hand brakes and started to slow.

But not Lilah.

It all happened so quickly.

In a second. Maybe less.

Becka saw the panic on Lilah's face.

"My brakes!" Lilah shrieked.

Becka squealed to a safe stop.

THE BEST FRIEND

Still picking up speed, Lilah flew over her handlebars into the intersection.

Becka shut her eyes.

Then she heard a loud *thump*.

Followed by a sickening *crunch*.

chapter
9

The sun was behind the trees now. The air carried a bitter winter chill.

The red lights on the top of the ambulances circled around and around.

Becka sat on the curb and stared as the red lights rolled over the ground, over the street, over Lilah's bent and mangled bike, still lying in the middle of the intersection.

Over the dark circle of blood in the street.

She heard a high-pitched voice talking rapidly, excitedly.

It was the truck driver, a young man in a denim work shirt and black jeans, with a red bandanna tied around his forehead. He was explaining to a grim-faced police officer what had happened. Gesturing wildly. His voice kept cracking as he talked.

Becka didn't look at him. She kept her gaze on the sweeping red ambulance lights.

56

The lights were comforting somehow. Hypnotic. So regular. So mechanical.

There were two ambulances there, Becka knew. And several black and white police cars.

The officers had wanted to talk to her, but she told them she wasn't ready to talk. She wanted to sit on the curb, on the cold, solid concrete, and watch the lights go around for a while.

Round and round.

She looked up in time to see the white-jacketed medics lift the stretcher into one of the ambulances.

The stretcher carrying Lilah.

The stretcher slid silently into the back of the ambulance.

Silent as death.

And then the doors were closed with a bang.

Lilah was alive.

The officers had told her that Lilah was alive.

She was unconscious. She was in bad shape.

But she was alive.

Becka shut her eyes. The sweeping red lights disappeared.

She heard the thud again.

And then she heard the crunch.

When she opened her eyes, she was panting, her heart thudding in her chest.

Will I hear those sounds every time I shut my eyes?

Becka realized she was standing. She didn't remember climbing to her feet.

But she was standing now.

Am I in shock?

The officer had muttered something about shock.

The red lights swept over her as she found herself walking toward the intersection.

Round and round.

I'm inside the red lights now.

So cold. So cold.

Will I ever be warm?

The red is cold.

And then she was lifting Lilah's bike. It had jerked to a stop and then slid into the intersection after Lilah. So bent. So totally wrecked. The seat as flat as a sheet of cardboard.

And the brakes—

Huh?

Becka's mouth dropped open. She stared hard at the mangled bike in her hands as the red lights swept over her. Then there was darkness, then the red light again.

One brake cable.

One of Lilah's brake cables.

It's *missing*, Becka saw.

She searched the street. There were no pieces there.

"My brakes!" Those were the words Lilah had screamed just before—before the bike slammed to a stop and she was thrown off.

Lilah had no rear wheel brakes. No brake cable to her back wheel.

The cable couldn't have come loose from *both* ends, Becka knew.

It couldn't have fallen off from both ends.

It had to have been removed.

"Hey—her rear brake cable—it's gone!" Becka shouted.

Did anyone hear her?

Did she really shout it?

Or did she just imagine that she had shouted it.

"Lilah's brake cable! Where is Lilah's brake cable?"

Was she talking to herself?

Wouldn't anyone listen to her?

Becka felt a hand on her shoulder. The hand was gentle. Protective.

She raised her eyes to the face of a young police officer. "Your friend is on her way to the hospital," he said softly, staring into her eyes with his wet blue ones. "Are you feeling better?"

"I don't know," Becka heard herself say.

"Would you like to go to the hospital too?" he asked, not blinking, not taking his eyes from hers. "Or would you like us to take you home?"

"Home," Becka said.

"Lilah is still unconscious," Becka whispered into the phone. "My mom just talked to her mom. The doctor said Lilah is stable."

"Stable? What does that mean?" Bill asked on the other end of the phone line.

Becka leaned over her desk. "I don't know. I guess that means she isn't getting any worse."

"And how are you doing?" Bill asked softly.

"Okay, I guess. Better. I keep getting chills. Mom keeps bringing me soup. Like I'm the one who's sick or something."

"You going to school tomorrow?" Bill asked.

"Yeah. I guess. I don't know." She uttered a loud sob. "I just can't believe it, Bill. Last night I was at Lilah's and we had such a good time. We were trimming her tree. Everyone was so happy, and now—"

"She'll be okay," Bill said soothingly. "I know she will."

Becka forced herself not to cry.

She hadn't cried at all. Not a tear.

Every time the urge hit her, she forced it back.

"You've been through a shock," Bill said.

"I'm keeping it together," she told him, her voice breaking.

"Lilah will be okay," Bill repeated.

He doesn't really believe it, Becka realized. He's trying to make me feel better.

He's sweet.

"Let's do something Saturday night," he urged. "Try to take our minds off everything."

"Okay," she agreed. The word tumbled out of her mouth. She was feeling so close to him now. He was being so understanding, so caring.

She just agreed without thinking.

"You'll do it?" He sounded very surprised.

"Yeah. I'll just sneak out," she told him. "It won't be any big deal. I'll tell my parents I'm going over to Trish's."

"Better let Trish in on it," Bill warned.

"Hey, I'm not stupid," she snapped.

"I know. But you're also not good at being sneaky."

"I can handle it," Becka assured him. "I really do need to get my mind off this. Poor Lilah." Again she choked back the tears.

"We'll go to a movie. A comedy," Bill promised. "We'll laugh all night. You'll see."

"I don't want to laugh all night," Becka insisted. "I just want—"

Becka suddenly had the feeling she wasn't alone.

She turned to her bedroom door—and cried out in alarm.

chapter
10

"*H*oney!" Becka cried. "How long have you been standing there? How did you get in here?"

Honey, her features tight with concern, stepped into Becka's bedroom.

"Listen, I've got to go. Bye," Becka said hurriedly into the phone. She hung up the receiver and stood up.

How much did Honey hear? Becka wondered.

"Becka, I heard the bad news. About Lilah," Honey cried. "You must feel *awful!*"

"Yes," Becka replied warily. "How did you get in here? Did my mom let you in?"

Honey nodded, then bounded across the room and wrapped Becka in a tight, protective hug.

"There, there," Honey said in a low voice that was meant to be soothing. "There there there there there."

"Honey, please—"

"You don't have to say anything," Honey said, not letting go of Becka. "I understand what you're feeling.

That's why I came running over the moment I heard. I knew my place was here."

"Well, really, Honey—" Becka struggled to free herself from Honey's tight hug.

Finally Honey let go and took a step back. She stared at Becka with an expression meant to be sympathetic and understanding.

"How awful for you, Becka. How awful. But you can let it out with me. You can be yourself, express your feelings without being embarrassed. That's what best friends are for, right?"

Grateful to be out of Honey's smothering hug, Becka made her way to the bed and dropped down onto her quilt with a weary sigh. "I really don't want to talk about it, Honey."

"Of course. I understand," Honey replied, crossing her arms in front of her, moving forward until she was standing directly over Becka.

An awkward silence followed.

Honey stared down at Becka who was sitting hunched over on her bed, her hands clasped tightly in her lap. Becka avoided Honey's stare, keeping her gaze focused on the evening darkness outside the window.

"You don't have to talk about it," Honey said finally. "It must have been such a shock. Such a horrible thing to witness."

"Yeah," Becka agreed, feeling her throat tighten.

"Didn't Lilah see the truck?" Honey asked.

Becka sighed. "Honey, I don't want to hurt your feelings. Really, I don't. But I really feel like being alone right now."

Honey's dark lips formed a small O of surprise, but she quickly recovered her concerned expression. "Of course you do, Becka. You were always like that. Even when we were little. You always had to sit and figure things out by yourself." Honey shook her head. "You were such a loner sometimes."

"Yeah, I guess," Becka said, feeling the urge to cry again and fighting it down.

"Well, I'm going home," Honey continued. "I just came to say that I'm here if you need me. You don't have Lilah anymore, so I want you to know I'm right here for you. Whenever."

You don't have Lilah anymore? Is that what Honey said?

"What did you say?" Becka cried.

"I said I'm right here for you," Honey said, retreating to the door.

No. I heard what you said. I heard what you said about Lilah.

You don't have Lilah anymore. Something about the way Honey said those words gave Becka a chill.

Suddenly, before Becka even realized it, hot tears were rolling down her cheeks, her shoulders were heaving, and she was sobbing, loud sobs of utter grief.

No! No! I don't want to cry! Becka thought.

But she couldn't stop herself now. Huddled on the bed, she let out loud, racking sobs, and covered her face with her hands.

"That's it. Let it all out." Honey's voice floated into Becka's consciousness.

She felt Honey's arm go around her shoulders. Honey was beside her on the bed now, hugging her, holding her, whispering soothingly. "There, there. Let it all out. I'm right here, Becka. It's okay. It's okay. I'm right here."

"Becka—?"

Another voice broke into Becka's consciousness.

A voice from the doorway.

Becka wiped her eyes with both hands and stared at the doorway. Trish was standing there, looking surprised and uncomfortable.

"Becka, are you okay?" Trish asked, taking a reluctant step into the room.

Becka cleared her throat, tried to reply.

Before she could answer Trish, Honey was on her feet and sailing across the room.

Grabbing Trish's elbow, Honey began to force her to leave. "Sorry, Trish, not now" Becka heard Honey say firmly. "Becka wants to be left alone."

Trish flashed Becka a helpless look. But Honey insisted. Holding her by the elbow, she led Trish out of the room.

Becka heard them both go down the stairs.

Then she buried her head in her hands and cried some more.

chapter

11

Becka put her hands behind Bill's neck and pulled his face to hers. She returned his kiss, a long, hard kiss, closing her eyes at first, then opening them to stare at the fogged-up windshield.

She liked the smell of his leather jacket.

She liked the softness of the long tangles of hair behind his head that she wrapped her fingers in, holding him close as they kissed.

He started to pull away, but she pulled his face to hers and found his lips for another kiss.

She didn't want to let him go.

Parked in her car on River Ridge, the windows all steamed, surrounded by the dark night, they were in their own world.

Safe and warm.

And silent.

Far below, the Conononka River flowed quietly, slowly, its waters choked with ice. Beyond the river stretched the town of Shadyside, lights twinkling through the trees on a clear, cold Saturday night.

But up on the high cliff known as River Ridge, pressed together in the front seat of the small car, Becka and Bill were alone. Far from everyone. Far from the people who would keep them apart.

After a long while Bill reached up and removed Becka's hands from the back of his head. "I—I can't breathe," he whispered, laughing giddily.

Becka sank back with a sigh. She pressed her forehead into the shoulder of his leather jacket.

"I like it here," she said softly, still tasting his lips on hers.

"Want to get out and look down at the town?" he asked, running a hand back through his hair, smoothing out some of the tangles.

"No. I don't want to move," Becka replied. "Ever."

She squeezed his hand, then held it. With his free hand, he absently drew circles in the steam on the passenger window.

"This is the first time I've been able to relax," she admitted. "I've been so crazed all week."

He turned to her, his expression serious. "Because of Lilah, you mean?"

"Because of everything," Becka told him, snuggling against his big shoulder. "Lilah. Honey. You."

"Me?"

"Having to sneak out tonight," she said softly. "Having to lie to my parents. I really hate it."

"Well, why don't you just tell them you're with me again?" Bill asked. "I mean, I'm not such a bad guy."

Becka didn't reply for a long while. Finally, she said, "You don't know my parents very well. Once they get an idea about someone in their heads—"

She let go of his hand and sank lower in the seat. "They'd probably give in after a while," she told him, staring at the dark windshield. "After a lot of screaming and yelling and arguing. And I just haven't felt—I haven't felt like screaming and yelling. Know what I mean?"

Bill nodded solemnly. "I guess. It's different at my house," he added thoughtfully. "There's never any screaming and yelling at my house because no one cares."

"Well, my parents care too much," Becka said, frowning. "Sometimes I wish they'd just back off, get out of my face. And then there's Honey." She groaned and ran her hands around the steering wheel.

"Honey is a pest, huh?"

"Pest isn't the word for it," Becka replied unhappily. "I—I've had such terrible thoughts about Honey. I mean, about Honey and Lilah's accident. I just don't know what to think. Honey is just so weird. So *weird!* She honestly believes we used to be best friends. But we weren't. We hardly knew each other. I really think she's made up a whole fantasy about how close we used to be. She believes her fantasy, and she's trying to force me to believe it too."

"She means well, doesn't she?" Bill asked, leaning close to her, his face showing his concern.

"I don't know," Becka told him. "Sometimes she's kind of sweet. I mean, she tries hard to be a good friend. But she just tries too hard."

"In other words, she's a pest," Bill said, snickering. He spelled out PEST in the window steam.

"It isn't funny," Becka said sharply. "Ever since— ever since Lilah's accident, Honey calls me three times a night. She drops over all the time. Every time I turn around, there she is, staring at me, giving me heartfelt sympathetic looks with those big gray eyes of hers."

Bill reached over and placed a hand tenderly on Becka's shoulder. "Calm down. You're getting yourself all crazy again."

"I can't help it," Becka wailed. "Honey is *making* me crazy! She's always hugging me. It's like she wants to smother me!"

"Becka, please—"

"She took my best blue top. You know—the silky one. She took it home to clean off a stain. And I never saw it again."

"Why don't you ask her for it?" Bill suggested.

"I did. She stared at me as if she didn't know what I was talking about!"

"Well, I don't get it," Bill said with growing impatience. "If Honey is so terrible, why don't you tell her not to come over? Why not tell her you don't want to be her friend?"

"That's easy to say," Becka replied heatedly. "But it's not so easy to do. You know how I hate to hurt people's feelings. I can't just say, 'Honey, get lost.'"

Bill shook his head. "It shouldn't be that hard to get rid of her."

"You don't know Honey. I don't think she'd even listen to me," Becka cried. "She's just so intense. She wants to be my best friend so badly. She's at the door every morning after breakfast. We have to go to school together. We sit together in homeroom and in several classes. She always hunts me down in the lunchroom, and we have to have lunch together. She even brings the same lunches I do!"

Bill laughed.

"It isn't funny!" Becka cried, giving him a shove. "Trish thinks it's really funny too. But it's not. It's *sick!*"

"Have you told any of this to your parents?" Bill asked, shifting in his seat to face her.

"Of course," Becka told him. "They think Honey is sweet. That's because Honey is always playing up to them, telling them how great they are, telling them how much she misses having a mother and how her father is always traveling and never around, and how she wishes she had a family like mine."

"Yuck." Bill put his finger down his throat.

"Yeah, I told you. It's *sick!*" Becka exclaimed. "But my parents just eat it up. And now, every time I start to complain about Honey, they don't want to hear about it. They even take *Honey's* side!"

"Calm down, Becka. Calm down," Bill urged with genuine concern. He reached over and took her hand. "You're shaking."

"I can't help it," Becka wailed. "She just makes me so crazy."

"How's Lilah doing?" he asked, deliberately changing the subject.

"She's better," Becka told him. "I visited the hospital this morning. She's doing real well. Better than the doctors expected. We had a nice talk, but . . ." Her voice trailed off.

"But what?" Bill demanded.

"Well, Lilah told me the strangest thing." Becka swallowed hard, then continued. "Lilah told me that Honey had been asking her questions about her bike. A day or two before the accident. You know. Questions about what kind of bike it was, how the brakes worked—stuff like that."

"So?" Bill asked, his expression puzzled.

"I don't know. I just think it's odd," Becka replied thoughtfully. "I didn't remember it until I talked to Lilah this morning. But Honey was at the bike rack when Lilah and I came for our bikes. She was examining a bike. Then she—"

"You don't think Honey did something to Lilah's bike, do you?" Bill asked skeptically.

The car suddenly filled with bright light as another car rolled past. Becka shielded her eyes. Darkness returned as the other car drove on.

"Maybe we should get going," Becka said nervously. She shivered.

"In a little while," Bill replied, staring at her intently. "First, tell me what you meant about Honey."

"Nothing," Becka replied uncomfortably. "I shouldn't have said it. I just—I've been thinking about it all day, picturing Honey there at the bike rack. And then . . ." Becka started to wipe the windshield clear with her hand.

Bill pulled her back in the seat. "Becka, come on," he scolded softly. "You really don't think Honey would try to kill Lilah just because Lilah was your friend."

"No, I guess not," Becka said uncertainly. "I don't know. I mean, I've been thinking so many crazy things. Honey just—she just— I'm a basket case, Bill. I really am!" Becka sobbed.

Bill reached for her, slid his arms around her, and held her close.

Becka stared out the windshield as he raised his face

to kiss her. Her eyes grew wider as she glimpsed something outside, something red behind a tree.

"Bill, she's there!" Becka cried, pulling away from him violently. "Honey! She's out there! She's watching us!"

Becka fumbled for the door handle.

"Wait—!" Bill cried.

He reached for her with both hands. But Becka pushed open the door and leapt out of the car.

"There she is! She followed us!" Becka screamed frantically, running to the tree.

chapter
12

Becka's breath steamed up in front of her as she ran through the darkness to the tree. Her heart pounded.

She was so angry, she felt she might explode.

How *dare* Honey?

What right did she have to follow Becka? To spy on her?

It was crazy. Just crazy.

Becka heard Bill's footsteps pounding the hard dirt behind her. "Becka, wait up!"

They both reached the tree at the same time.

"Honey?" Becka called breathlessly. "Honey?"

She gasped in a mouthful of cold air.

And stared at the red kerchief. The red kerchief dangling from a skinny, low tree branch.

How could she have thought that that red kerchief was Honey?

Bill grabbed the kerchief and pulled it down. He held it up to Becka.

She expected him to laugh at her. But Bill's face was serious, his features narrowed in concern.

"Becka, I'm really worried about you," he said softly. He lowered the kerchief, then let it drop to the ground. "You've got to find a way to calm down," he said, staring at her intently.

"I know," Becka replied, trembling all over. "But what can I do, Bill? What can I do?"

Becka groaned and tried to sit up.

Her head felt as if it weighed two tons. She sank back onto her pillow.

She reached for the thermometer, then remembered she had just taken her temperature ten minutes before. It had been 101.6.

What time was it, anyway?

She struggled to focus on the clock radio beside her bed. A little past noon. Monday afternoon.

She had felt a little strange Sunday night. A little queasy. A little achy.

When she had tried to get out of bed Monday morning, she knew at once she was really sick. The flu, probably. Or some kind of virus. Something was always going around.

"I wish I could stay home and take care of you," her mom had said, bringing her tea and buttered toast on a tray. Becka forced down some of the tea. She couldn't eat the toast.

"That's okay, Mom. I'm not a little kid. I can manage," she had said. Her head throbbed as if someone were inside, pounding with a hammer to get out. "I'm just going to sleep all day."

"I'll try to come home early," Mrs. Norwood said,

frowning. "Drink plenty of liquids, okay? Here. Wait a sec. I'll get you some Tylenol."

Becka's mom didn't return for what seemed a long while. Becka lay on her back, feeling uncomfortable but too weak to change her position. She stared up at the ceiling, trying to remember what was going on in school.

"Here are the Tylenols. Take them with this juice." Her mother leaned over her, holding a small juice glass and two pills. "That was Honey downstairs," she said, as Becka sat up with great effort. "She wanted to come up, but I told her how sick you are."

"Thanks," Becka said weakly. She choked down the two pills and handed the juice glass back to her mother.

"Honey said she'd be sure to bring you your homework after school," Mrs. Norwood said. "She's such a considerate girl, isn't she."

"Who needs homework?" Becka muttered bitterly. She sank back onto her pillow with a loud groan.

"Does anything hurt in particular?" Mrs. Norwood asked, biting her lower lip.

"Everything hurts," Becka moaned.

"Well, sleep all day then," Mrs. Norwood said, placing a cool hand on Becka's hot forehead. "Ooh. Pretty hot. I'll call you later. Be sure to drink a lot. If you're not better by tomorrow, we'd better call Doctor Klein."

Becka's mom disappeared out the door.

Becka stared up at the ceiling for a long while. Then she shifted onto her side.

I'm dying, she thought. I feel so bad.

She fell into a restless sleep. Her mother called

around eleven, waking her up. After mumbling something to her, Becka padded down to the kitchen, poured herself a tall glass of apple juice, then returned to her bed.

The afternoon passed in a feverish blur. Half awake, half asleep, Becka tossed uncomfortably, feeling hot and sweaty, and then pulling the covers up to her chin when she had the chills.

She had wild dreams, vivid with glaringly bright colors.

Dreams with chase scenes.

She was running, running desperately, trying to escape from she didn't know what.

The dreams collided with other dreams.

She and Lilah were riding the same bike. Then Honey was running alongside.

Then all three of them were on the bike and the bike toppled over.

Such strange dreams, disturbing dreams.

One right after the other.

The phone rang at three-fifteen.

It took three rings for Becka to realize what the sound was.

"Hello?" Her voice was choked. She coughed hard to clear her throat.

"Oh. You're home," a familiar voice said on the other end.

"Trish?"

"I didn't think you'd be home," Trish said.

"Huh? Why not?"

"Well, I thought maybe you were in the hospital, Becka. I've been so worried. I couldn't wait to get home to call you."

The room was spinning around Becka. Gripping the phone tightly, she closed her eyes and sank back onto the pillow.

"Trish, why on earth would I be in the hospital?"

"Well," Trish hesitated on the other end of the line. "Honey told everyone about your breakdown."

chapter
13

*B*ecka's throat tightened.

She suddenly felt cold all over. Chilled.

"Trish, what did you say?" she asked in a quivering voice.

"Well, when you weren't in homeroom this morning, I asked Honey where you were. And she said she had really bad news. She said you'd had a breakdown."

"Huh? She *did?*"

"Yeah, she said it was because of Lilah's accident."

Becka tried to talk, but the words wouldn't come out. She suddenly realized she was gripping the phone receiver so tightly her hand was aching.

"Honey said you totally freaked out," Trish continued. "She was telling everyone. I was sure you were in a hospital or something. I was so worried, Becka."

"I don't believe it!" Becka managed to cry in a high-pitched voice. "I don't believe it!"

"So, you didn't have a breakdown?" Trish asked timidly.

"Trish, I have a virus," Becka told her. "A stupid virus. That's all."

"Whew." Trish exhaled noisily.

"Why would Honey do that?" Becka cried. "Why?"

"Beats me," Trish replied. "She must have gotten mixed up, I guess. I'm just so glad. I mean, I'm not glad you have a virus. I'm just glad you're not—"

"Is she crazy?" Becka interrupted. "Is she some kind of compulsive liar, or something?"

"I don't know," Trish said. "I don't know what to say. Honey is strange. That's for sure. Listen, Becka, I have good news about my party."

"Party?" Becka's head was spinning. Her thoughts were all jumbled, falling one on top of the other the way her fever dreams had.

"You know. My Christmas party."

"Oh, right."

"I'm sure you'll be feeling okay by then," Trish continued. "The good news is my parents agreed to go out. So we won't have anyone in our faces, watching our every move."

"That's great," Becka replied weakly, trying to concentrate.

"That means my parents won't know that Bill is at the party," Trish continued. "They won't be able to tell your parents. So you're safe. No problem!"

"Great," Becka muttered.

"Gee, you sound terrible," Trish said sympathetically. "Can I bring you anything? Chicken soup. A hot fudge sundae . . ."

Becka groaned in reply.

"I talked to Lilah. Last night," Trish said. "She

sounded pretty good, considering what she's been through."

"Yeah. I visited her yesterday," Becka said. "She's doing really well. She's desperate to get out of the hospital now."

"Poor thing," Trish replied, tsk-tsking. "It's going to be a really long time. Months maybe. Then lots of therapy for her legs. But at least she'll be okay someday. I feel so bad that she's going to miss my party, but you'll be there, right?"

"I'll be there," Becka groaned. "Even if I'm dying." She kicked off the sheet and blanket. She felt hot and sweaty again. Her mouth felt as dry as cotton.

"So you haven't seen Honey today?" Trish asked.

"How could I?" Becka snapped. "I've been lying in this bed all day, moaning and groaning."

"Wait till you see her."

"Huh? What about her?" Becka demanded.

"I don't want to spoil the surprise," Trish said mysteriously.

"Surprise? Trish?"

"I've got to run," Trish said. "Call me if there's anything I can do. Glad you're okay. I mean, you know."

She hung up.

Becka stared at the receiver for a long time, then finally dropped it back.

She sat up, feeling dizzy. She took a long sip of the apple juice she had carried up earlier. It was warm and tasted sour to her.

She shook the thermometer and put it in her mouth.

I know I have a fever, she thought. Tomorrow's the last day of school before the vacation. But I won't be able to go.

Her temperature was still a little over 101.

She replaced the thermometer and fluffed her pillow. She was just lying back on the pillow when she heard footsteps on the stairs.

"Hi, Becka, it's me!" Honey called up cheerfully. "The front door was unlocked, so I let myself in. How are you feeling? I've been worried about you all day."

Becka jerked upright.

Her entire body tensed.

I'm going to ask her right out if she's been spreading horrible lies about me, Becka decided.

Honey floated into the room. "Hi. You feeling better?"

Becka's mouth dropped open in shock.

She stared wide-eyed at Honey.

"Like it?" Honey asked, striking a pose.

Becka couldn't speak.

Honey twirled around in a circle.

Her long mane of thick auburn hair was gone.

She has my short haircut, Becka realized. *She's cut her hair to look exactly like mine!*

chapter

14

After Honey finally went home, Becka
drifted in and out of sleep. She managed to down two
pieces of buttered toast with a cup of tea for dinner.
Then she fell back into a troubled sleep while staring
at her television.

The jangling of the phone stirred her from her
unpleasant dreams. Groggily, she reached for it, struggling to focus on the bedtable clock. Ten thirty-three.

"Hello?" Her voice came out still choked with
sleep. Her head ached. Everything ached.

"Becka, it's me again. Honey."

Who else?

"Honey, I was asleep." Groaning, Becka raised
herself on the pillow.

"Oh. Sorry. I just had to call one more time,
Becka."

Honey had already called twice since that afternoon.

"I'm feeling a little better, I think," Becka whispered. "But I don't know if I'll go to school tomorrow or not."

"I didn't call about that," Honey replied, her voice quivering. "I just can't stop thinking about— I just can't *stand* it that you think I said those horrible things about you in school today."

"Honey, we've been over this already," Becka said, sighing wearily. Her mouth felt dry. Balancing the phone on her shoulder, she reached for the water glass on the bedside table.

"I know we have. I'm sorry," Honey replied. "But I have to know that you believe me, Becka. You have to believe me. I never told anyone you had a breakdown. That's just too stupid. Why would I do a thing like that?"

"Honey, really," Becka tried to cut in, but Honey insisted on continuing.

"I never said those things," Honey said emotionally. "Really. Trish lied. I never told her or anyone else that you had a breakdown. Trish is a liar, Becka. You've *got* to believe me."

Becka's head felt as heavy as a bowling ball. She dropped back onto the pillow and shut her eyes. "Honey, I'm sick. I really have to sleep. Please—"

"Just say you believe me," Honey insisted.

Becka took a deep breath. "Okay. I believe you."

Anything to get her off the phone.

"Oh, thanks," Honey cried gratefully. "Thanks, Becka. I knew you wouldn't believe such a dumb story. It's just that we had such a bad visit this afternoon. I mean, I could tell you didn't like my haircut, and—"

"I didn't say I didn't like it," Becka groaned. "I—it was just a shock, that's all. I didn't expect—"

"You mean you really do *like* it?" Honey asked.

"Yes, you look great," Becka told her.

"But do you like it?" Honey pleaded.

"Yes. It's wonderful," Becka lied. "Listen, Honey, I really feel lousy. I've got to get back to sleep, okay?"

"Okay. I feel much better about everything. I won't call again, Becka, but I'm here if you need me, all right? I'll call tomorrow morning. I hope you'll be well enough to go to school. It's the last day, you know."

"I know," Becka said. "Good night." She replaced the receiver without waiting for a reply.

Honey is driving me crazy! Becka thought.

Crazy!

She pulled the pillow over her and pressed it down over her chest.

What am I going to do about her?

She gripped the pillow tightly, holding on as if her life depended on it.

What am I going to do?

Honey had upset her so much, it took Becka nearly two hours to fall back to sleep.

Becka undid the combination lock and pulled open her locker door. She reached up to get a looseleaf binder from the shelf.

"Ow." Her head throbbed when she looked up.

She still felt weak. She probably should have stayed in bed one more day. But she didn't want to miss the last day of school before Christmas break.

"Oh! Becka, you're here!"

Hearing a cry of surprise behind her, Becka turned

around. "Oh, hi, Cari," she said, balancing her backpack on one raised knee and struggling to stuff the binder into it.

It was her friend Cari Taylor, a petite, pretty girl with bright blue eyes and straight blond hair tied to one side in a short ponytail. Cari had the locker next to Becka's.

"I—I didn't think you'd be here," Cari said awkwardly, studying Becka intently. "I mean, I heard . . ."

"I had a virus or something," Becka said, frowning. Her math textbook slipped out and fell to the floor. "I'm a little better today."

Cari blushed. "I'm glad," she said. "I mean, I'm not glad you were sick. I—I just heard you were *really* sick."

"Who said that?" Becka snapped, bending to retrieve the math text. Her head throbbed painfully again as she reached down for it.

Cari shrugged. "Some kids said you'd had a breakdown," she said, lowering her voice to a whisper.

Becka shook her head. "No, I'm okay. Really."

"A stupid rumor, I guess," Cari said, obviously embarrassed. "Who knows how these things get started?"

"I know," Becka muttered bitterly.

She zipped up her backpack. The first bell rang. Locker doors slammed all down the long hallway. Combination locks clicked. Kids made their way, talking and laughing, to their homerooms.

Becka snapped her lock and began walking down the hall with Cari.

Honey is a total liar, Becka realized, feeling her

anger grow. Honey did tell everyone I had a break-down.

She saw a cluster of kids waiting for the library to open. Their faces filled with surprise when they saw Becka pass by.

They must have heard the rumor too.

"What are you doing this vacation?" Becka asked Cari, trying to force her mind off Honey.

"Oh, Reva Dalby invited me to go skiing with her and her dad," Cari answered, smiling. "They go skiing every Christmas, just about. I can't wait. I've never been to Aspen. It should be really awesome at Christmastime."

They stopped outside Cari's homeroom. "What are you doing?" Cari asked.

"Not much," Becka said. "We always stay around home. We have a million relatives to visit. And you know Trish is having a big party Saturday."

The second bell rang.

"Yeah. I'm sorry I have to miss it. Bye. Have a good one!" Cari cried, ducking into the classroom. And then she added, "I'm glad you're okay."

Becka dashed across the hall to her homeroom, tossed her backpack to the floor, and slid into her seat.

Is it just my imagination? she wondered. Or is everyone staring at me?

Did Honey tell everyone in the room that I had a breakdown?

She turned to look at Honey in the seat beside her. It was still a shock, a horrible shock, to see Honey's short auburn hair, an exact copy of Becka's haircut.

She's wearing my silky blue top, Becka realized angrily. And she has my parrot pin on the collar.

Honey had a book open in her lap. She closed it and smiled at Becka.

"How are you feeling, Becka? You look so pale."

"Not so great," Becka muttered, frowning.

"I told you before we left your house you should've stayed home," Honey scolded. "I would've brought you all your homework. I would have taken care of everything for you. Everything."

What am I going to do about her? Becka asked herself miserably.

The question had become an obsession, an endless refrain.

What am I going to do?

"What am I going to do, Trish?" Becka asked. It came out sounding more like a plea than a question.

Trish shivered and zipped her wool parka up to the collar. She stuffed her hands into her coat pockets and picked up her pace to keep up with Becka, her boots sinking into the soft ground.

It was lunch period. But Becka didn't have any appetite. After much pleading, she persuaded a reluctant Trish to go for a walk behind the school.

It was a cold, gray day, heavy clouds hovering low. The air was wet. It smelled as if it might start to snow any minute.

"You shouldn't be walking around outside. You're sick," Trish scolded.

"I had to get out," Becka told her. "I just couldn't bear the idea of sitting in the lunchroom, trying to choke down a sandwich with Honey staring across the table at me."

They followed the walkway that led behind the

stadium. The football field was silent and empty. One of the goalposts had been knocked over in a strong wind a few weeks before.

"Honey is ruining my life," Becka moaned. "What am I going to do?"

"Why don't we murder her?" Trish suggested.

chapter
15

*B*ecka stopped and gaped at Trish.

Trish laughed.

"Oh, Trish," Becka cried, shaking her head. "Honey has me so messed up, I actually believed you. I thought you were serious."

"No, it was a joke," Trish said, pulling her green wool cap down lower over her head, pushing her red curls inside it. "You really *are* in bad shape, Becka."

They had circled the stadium. Behind them stretched Shadyside Park, wintry and bare, dark, leafless trees shivering in the wind. They turned away from the park and, with the wind at their backs, began to make their way slowly toward the student parking lot.

"I can't believe I let you talk me out of lunch. I'm starving!" Trish complained.

"You're not being very helpful," Becka said. "I mean, about Honey."

"And I'm freezing," Trish continued, ignoring Becka. "This cold air is making my braces freeze up!"

Trish stopped first, her mouth dropping open in surprise. She raised an arm to halt Becka.

Becka followed her friend's gaze to the parking lot.

There was Honey. She was walking slowly between the two rows of cars. Walking with a boy.

He had his arm around her shoulders.

They stopped and kissed.

"I don't believe it," Becka whispered, moving behind Trish as if to hide.

They stared in silence as Honey leaned her back against a car, and she and the boy kissed some more.

"Who's she with?" Becka whispered.

"I can't see his face," Trish replied. "We're too far away."

Staying close to the metal chain-link fence that lined the football field, they made their way closer to the parking lot.

"Oh, wow! It's Eric!" Trish declared.

"Eric who?" Becka demanded. "*My* Eric?"

"Yeah." Trish nodded

Becka grabbed the metal wires of the fence and squeezed till her hands hurt.

"Well, you broke up with him," Trish said. "I guess she has a right—"

"Trish! Look at her!" Becka cried heatedly. "Her hair is cut like mine. She's wearing a down jacket just like mine. She's wearing my blue top that she took home and never returned. And my parrot pin, the enamel pin that Bill gave me. And she's standing there in the parking lot, kissing my old boyfriend!"

"Becka—"

"That's sick! It's just *sick!*"

"Becka, you're screaming. Calm down, okay? Just chill!" Trish grabbed Becka's shoulder and stared at her, concerned.

Becka hadn't even realized she was screaming. She took a deep breath and held it. She let go of the fence and shoved her frozen hands into her jacket pockets.

"I knew we should've stayed inside," Trish said, frowning.

"What am I going to do?" Becka asked once again, forcing her voice to stay low and steady. She returned her eyes to the parking lot. Honey and Eric were walking arm in arm along the walk, toward Becka and Trish.

"You're just going to have to be honest with her," Trish said, fiddling with her wool cap.

"Honest? What do you mean?" Becka demanded.

"You're going to have to tell her you don't want to be friends with her."

Two large blackbirds swooped low overhead, cawing loudly, on their way to the park.

I wish I could fly away with them, Becka thought miserably, watching Eric and Honey approach.

"But if I tell Honey that, I don't know what she'll do," Becka said. "She's so emotional. She's crazy. She's really crazy. I mean, I even think she caused Lilah's accident."

Trish raised her eyes to Becka's, her expression troubled. "Don't you totally freak over this, Becka," she warned quietly. "Don't get totally paranoid. Honey may be a terrible pest. And a copycat. But if you start making crazy accusations . . ." She didn't finish her thought.

"You don't know her as well as I do," Becka argued.

Glancing up ahead, she saw that Eric had suddenly turned around and was hurrying back to the school building. Honey was approaching quickly, jogging toward them, waving.

Eric must be embarrassed or something, Becka thought.

"Hi, Becka!" Honey called. She stopped in front of Becka, breathing hard, her breath steaming up from her mouth, a big smile on her face.

"Hi," Becka muttered with an obvious lack of enthusiasm.

"What are you doing out here?" Honey asked.

"Just talking with Trish."

"Oh." Honey seemed to notice Trish for the first time. "Hi."

Trish nodded.

"Can I join you?" Honey asked Becka.

Becka shook her head. "Not now, Honey. I really want to have a private talk with Trish."

"Private?"

"Yeah," Becka replied coldly.

Honey's mouth dropped open. Her gray eyes narrowed. "What's going on, Becka?" she demanded, sounding hurt. "There's nothing you can't share with your best friend."

"That's why I'm talking to Trish!" Becka said pointedly.

There, Becka thought. That should be clear enough. Now maybe Honey will take the hint.

Honey's expression became a blank. It revealed no emotion, but her face turned bright red.

She shoved her large hands into the pockets of her

down jacket and turned away quickly. "Talk to you later," she called behind her and began jogging to the school.

"That was subtle," Trish said dryly. She chuckled. "I think Honey got the point."

Becka didn't smile. She suddenly found herself overcome with regret, with fear. "I shouldn't have been so blunt," she said, her voice a whisper.

"Yes, you should," Trish insisted. "You've been patient for so long. It was the only way."

"You'd better be careful, Trish," Becka said, biting her thumb.

"Huh? What do you mean?"

"You'd better be careful. I know it sounds crazy. I know it sounds paranoid. But I really think Honey could be dangerous. If she's jealous of you, if she starts to really resent you, she might try to do something."

Trish laughed and shook her head. "Chill out, Becka," she scolded. "I mean, really. What can she do?"

chapter

16

"*T*ake care of yourself," Trish said as they stepped into the warmth of the building. "You *can't* miss my Christmas party Saturday."

"I'll be okay," Becka said, shivering. "Talk to you later, Trish. Thanks for walking with me."

Becka waved to her friend, then turned and headed down the crowded corridor to her locker. She still felt achy and sick.

I probably shouldn't have stayed out in the cold like that, she thought.

She waved to some kids, then turned the corner and kept walking. Glancing at a wall clock, she saw that there were still ten minutes left in the lunch period.

Good, she thought. *It'll give me time to go to the girls' room and get myself together.*

After stepping around a group of guys who were huddled together, laughing about something, slapping one another high-fives, she stopped in front of her locker.

"Oh." To her surprise, the locker door was open a crack.

I *know* I locked it, she told herself.

She pulled open the door and gasped.

"Becka, what's the matter?"

Becka turned to see Cari Taylor beside her, starting to open her locker. "Look," Becka said, pointing.

"Oh, wow!" Cari exclaimed, moving over to peer into Becka's locker. "Someone trashed everything!"

"Everything," Becka uttered weakly.

Her textbooks, usually neatly stacked on the top shelf, had been tossed to the locker floor. Her binders had been torn apart, pages pulled out. The wool scarf she kept in the locker had been balled up under a jumble of loose papers. The note cards for her research project were scattered over everything.

"How *gross!*" Cari exclaimed. "Who would do this?" She put a hand on Becka's trembling shoulder. "You've got to report this."

"Yeah, I know," Becka replied.

A wave of nausea swept over her. She forced herself to look away from the mess.

"Who would do this?" Cari repeated.

Several other kids had hurried over to see what the commotion was.

I know who did it, Becka thought bitterly.

I don't have to guess.

Honey did it.

Of all the stupid, babyish things!

Just because I hurt her feelings, she had to pay me back instantly by messing up all my stuff.

"Aaaagh!" Becka uttered an exasperated cry and lurched away from the noisy crowd that had gathered in front of her locker.

"Becka, where are you going?" Cari called after her.

"To the girls' room," Becka shouted.

She pushed her way through a group of cheerleaders, in their uniforms for some reason, and hurried down the noisy hall, voices echoing in her ears.

Into the girls' room at the end of the corridor.

Breathing hard.

Gray light flooded in through the frosted glass of the tall window.

Honey stood at the sink.

Still in her down jacket.

"Oh!" Becka cried out.

Honey turned to her, also surprised. "Hi." She turned off the water faucets and pulled a paper towel from the dispenser beside the mirror.

"Honey!" Becka screamed. She felt herself going out of control. She couldn't help it. She'd been holding back too long. *"How could you?"*

Honey's eyes opened wide in bewilderment. She stopped drying her hands. "Huh?"

"How could you?"

"What, Becka? How could I what?"

"You know, you liar!" Becka shrieked.

Honey crumpled the paper towel in her hand and let it fall to the tile floor. "Becka, you're screaming," she said, her bewildered expression turning to one of concern. "Are you okay?"

"No, Honey, I'm not okay!" Becka cried, taking angry steps toward Honey. "I'm not okay, and you know I'm not okay."

Honey, alarmed, took a step back toward the stalls. She raised her hands in a gesture of surrender.

"How *could* you?" Becka screamed, straining her throat. Her hands were balled into tight fists at her sides. Her temples throbbed. The white light from the window shimmered in front of her.

Honey sighed. She stood tensely, returning Becka's stare. "Really, Becka, you'll have to calm down. I don't know what you're talking about. I really don't."

"Liar," Becka said accusingly. "I'm talking about my locker, of course."

"What about your locker?" Honey asked, innocent as innocent could be.

Becka took a breath, started to reply, found herself speechless. Too angry to make a sound.

"Why are you picking on me today?" Honey demanded, tears forming in the corners of her gray eyes. Her chin trembled. "Tell me, Becka. What have I done?"

Becka leaned against a sink, squeezing her hands on the cool porcelain, trying to force herself back in control.

"You were so mean to me outside by the football field," Honey exclaimed, two large tears running down her scarlet cheeks. "And now you come barging in here screaming at me for no reason." Honey uttered a loud sob. "Why, Becka? Why are you picking on me?"

"Just stay away from my things," Becka managed to say through clenched teeth. "Stay away."

"Oh." Honey wiped the tears off with her hands. "I get it. You mean Eric. You saw me with Eric."

"No," Becka snapped.

"You're angry because I'm with Eric now," Honey interrupted. "But that's not fair, Becka. You broke up with him."

"I don't mean Eric," Becka cried. She realized she was trembling all over.

She took a deep breath and held it.

Gripping the sink, she closed her eyes.

But the trembling didn't stop.

"I don't mean Eric," she repeated.

"You gave him up. Now he's with me," Honey insisted. She turned to the mirror and examined herself, wiping another tear off her cheek.

Is she checking out her hairdo? Becka thought bitterly. *My* hairdo!

Is she getting tear stains on her blue blouse? *My* blue blouse!

"I'm telling you, Honey, it isn't Eric. It's everything else!" Becka said.

"Now what are you talking about?" Honey asked, bewildered.

"Everything else," Becka repeated. "I want you to stay away from my house! Stay away from my room! Stay away from my friends!"

Honey cringed, a wounded expression twisting her features. "You, you can't talk to me that way, Becka! You can't!" Her expression quickly became angry, her gray eyes burning into Becka's. "I'm your best friend! Your *best* friend!"

With a desperate cry, Honey reached into her jacket pocket. After a brief struggle, she pulled out a silver pistol.

"Honey, no! Put that down!" Becka shrieked.

Her face twisted in anger, Honey raised the pistol, aimed it at Becka's chest, and pulled the trigger.

*B*ecka uttered a high-pitched scream.

A stream of cold water shot out of the gun onto the front of Becka's jacket.

Honey laughed.

"Come on, Becka," she scolded, shaking her head. "Whatever happened to your sense of humor?"

Becka, breathing hard, glared silently back at Honey.

"I gotcha again," Honey boasted. She squeezed the trigger of the silver squirt gun, sending a spray of water to the mirror. She grinned at Becka.

Why is she grinning? Becka asked herself angrily. Hasn't she heard a word I said?

Becka stared at the water dripping down the mirror.

"Come on, Becka," Honey repeated. "Don't you remember how we both used to carry squirt guns all the time? Those red plastic ones? Remember? We used to shoot each other every time Miss Martin turned her back?"

"No," Becka said softly.

Honey laughed. "We'd be totally soaked by the end of the day, remember?"

"No," Becka repeated more loudly.

"Becka, don't you remember?"

"No! No! No!" Now Becka was screaming. "No, Honey, we didn't! We didn't! We didn't have squirt guns! We didn't squirt each other!"

"Of course we did," Honey insisted, still smiling. "You just don't remember."

"No! No!" Becka screamed, out of control.

The bell rang.

"No!"

She turned and ran, pushing the door open with her shoulder, out into the crowded hall, still running, past startled faces, past kids calling her name, running faster. *No, no, no!* The word repeating endlessly in her head.

Running blindly against the tide of kids.

Running breathlessly.

Wishing she could run forever.

"Whoa," Bill greeted Becka at his front door, surprised as he pushed open the glass storm door and stared at her under the yellow porch light. He was wearing a faded maroon and gray Shadyside High sweatshirt over jeans. He was barefoot despite the cold.

"Hi," Becka said shyly, biting her lower lip. "Okay if I come in? I was going to call first, but I thought my mom might overhear."

"Yeah. Sure." He scratched the front of his long, scraggly hair.

Unzipping her jacket, she pushed past him into the

narrow hallway. The house was hot, almost steamy, and smelled of fried grease. "Anybody home?" she asked, peering into the dark living room.

"No. Just us mice," he told her. He took her jacket, carried it into the living room, and tossed it onto a chair. Then he clicked on a table light and motioned for her to sit down on the navy blue corduroy couch.

"My dad's still at work," he said, dropping down beside her, pushing his hair back off his face. "My mom's grocery shopping, I think."

Becka sniffed. "What's that smell?"

"We had hamburgers for dinner," he told her. "Did you eat?"

Becka nodded. "I wasn't very hungry."

He crossed his legs and stretched an arm behind her on the back of the couch. "What did you tell your mom?"

"That I was going to Trish's," Becka replied. She sighed. "I had to talk to someone. I'm so messed up, I can't . . ."

He lowered his arm and put it around her shoulders. He started to pull her close, but she edged away.

"No, I have to talk," she told him.

He obediently pulled his hand away.

Without taking a breath, Becka unleashed a torrent of words. "I don't know what to do, Bill. It's Honey. She's driving me crazy. Totally crazy. I really think I'm freaking out because of her. I can't think straight. I can't do my homework. I can't do anything."

"What did she do now?" Bill asked, frowning.

"Everything!" Becka exclaimed. "She doesn't leave me alone. And when I tell her I want her to go away, when I tell her to back off, she just laughs. Like it's some kind of joke. Like she doesn't believe I could be serious."

Bill's expression showed concern. He stared intently at Becka. "Becka, you've got to calm down," he started.

"How can I?" she cried shrilly. "Have you *seen* her, Bill? She's wearing my clothes. She has my hairdo. She's going with Eric. She—she—"

"Really," Bill said softly, putting a hand on Becka's shoulder. "Look at you, Becka. You're shaking. You're making yourself crazy."

"I'm not! Honey is!" Becka shrieked. "What am I going to do?"

Bill edged toward the arm of the couch. Becka knew he hated it when she screamed and lost control. He just didn't know how to deal with her being so high-strung.

But she couldn't help it.

She was too upset. She needed to confide in him now. She needed his help.

"I'm really worried about you," he said quietly, lowering his eyes to the worn carpet. "I—I don't know what to say."

Becka took a deep breath and held it. She didn't want to start to cry.

Bill hated crying even more than shouting.

"Have you talked to your mom about Honey?" Bill asked.

Becka nodded. "Yeah. But she thinks I'm exaggerating. Every time she sees Honey, Honey is on her best behavior. She's always flattering my mom and telling her how she wishes she was part of our family. My mom keeps telling me to give Honey a chance, that Honey is lonely. Mom says Honey will make other friends after she's been here for a while, and then she won't pester me so much."

"But you don't believe that?" Bill asked, working his big toe into a small hole in the carpet in front of the couch.

Becka shook her head. "No. Of course not," she replied shrilly. "Mom and I got into the worst fight over Honey. I know it was childish of me, but I just couldn't stand for her to take Honey's side."

Bill concentrated on digging his toe into the hole. He didn't say anything.

"Trish says I have to get tough," Becka continued. "Trish says I have to be mean. I have to tell Honey exactly how I feel. I have to tell Honey that I don't want her coming over, that I don't want to be her friend."

Bill snickered. "Trish is tough," he muttered.

"Well, at lunch period today I sort of tried it," Becka told him. "Trish and I were walking by the football field. And Honey was in the parking lot with Eric. She wanted to join Trish and me. But I said I wanted to talk to Trish alone. I thought maybe Honey got the point, but then—"

"Oh, wow," Bill interrupted. "Did you hear about the guys who broke into the school during lunch period today?"

"Guys? What guys?"

Bill shrugged. "Some guys. They ran through the halls, trashing lockers. You know Gary Brandt? They tore up all his textbooks and stole his letter jacket. Some other kids had their lockers trashed too. It was unbelievable. Then the guys ran out the front door and got away."

"Oh, no!" Becka sank back into the couch and stared up at the ceiling.

"What?" Bill asked. "What's wrong?"

"My locker was trashed too," Becka said weakly. "And I didn't know it was vandals. I accused Honey."

Bill said something, but Becka didn't hear him. She stared up at the ceiling, stared at the gray smoke detector near the wall, stared without seeing, without hearing.

I accused Honey. No wonder she looked at me like that in the girls' room. No wonder she didn't know what I was talking about. And then she accused me of picking on her. Picking on her for no reason.

And it turns out Honey was right.

Bill was talking, but Becka didn't hear him. He seemed far away, miles away, his voice a distant murmur.

I screamed at Honey, Becka recalled. I screamed at her and threatened her. Honey tried to make a joke of it. She tried to get me to lighten up with the squirt gun.

But I acted like a total psycho!

Like a crazy person.

"Am I being unfair to Honey?" Becka asked aloud. She lowered her eyes to Bill. The room came quickly back into focus.

"Maybe," he said thoughtfully.

"You think so?"

Becka felt completely confused now. She had sneaked over to Bill's to confide in him, so certain that she was right about Honey. So certain that Honey was her enemy.

That Honey was determined to ruin her life.

But now . . .

Becka's mind was thrown into turmoil.

Honey probably thinks *I'm* crazy, she thought, feeling very embarrassed.

I'm the one who flies off the handle and accuses her of things she didn't do.

I'm the one who screams and cries.

She's the calm one. She's the one who tries to calm *me* down.

She puts up with me because she wants to be my friend.

"Maybe you are being a little unfair to Honey." Bill's words cut through Becka's painful thoughts. "Honey isn't that bad. In fact, she's kind of cute."

"Huh?"

Becka sat up straight and glared at Bill. "You think she's cute?"

Bill realized immediately that he'd made a mistake. "I just said kind of," he muttered.

"You shouldn't take her side," Becka said, feeling herself go out of control. Fighting it. Fighting it.

"I didn't," Bill quickly insisted. "Now, listen, Becka—"

"You shouldn't take her side, even joking around."

"I didn't," Bill repeated, rolling his eyes.

"Did she ever come on to you?" Becka demanded. "Huh?"

"You heard me. Did Honey ever come on to you?"

Bill turned his eyes back to the carpet. "Maybe," he said softly. "But it was no big deal."

Becka left Bill's house a few minutes later, feeling more unsettled and troubled than when she had arrived.

Bill had pulled her close to him on the couch, had wrapped his arms around her, had kissed her. Long kisses. Kisses she normally would have enjoyed.

But not tonight.

As she pressed her mouth against his, her eyes closed, she thought about Honey.

She saw the squirt gun. Honey's short haircut. The enamel parrot pin.

She saw the girls' room. Honey standing by the sink. The surprised look on Honey's face when Becka began accusing her.

Go away, Honey, Becka thought. Please, go away.

She pulled herself away from Bill, left him with a startled expression on his face. He reached for her. Missed. She grabbed her jacket and hurried out the door.

She drove around for a while, thinking, thinking.

But not feeling any more settled.

She thought about dropping in on Trish, but decided against it.

It was nearly ten o'clock when she pulled up the drive and parked the car in the garage.

The cold air stung her face as she made her way to the back door.

When she pulled it open, she saw that someone was huddled at the kitchen table, her back to the door, waiting for Becka.

"Oh!" Becka cried.

chapter

18

"Mom!" Becka cried. "Why are you sitting there?"

Mrs. Norwood turned around slowly. She didn't smile.

"Mom, are you okay?"

"Have a good time?" Becka's mother asked coldly. She pulled herself to a standing position.

"No," Becka replied, bewildered. "I . . . uh . . ."

"Were you at Bill's?" Mrs. Norwood asked angrily. She placed her hands at her waist and stared hard at Becka, searching her face.

"Mom, I don't get it," Becka replied, dread forming in the pit of her stomach. She busied herself pulling off her jacket, thinking hard, trying to decide how much her mother knew, trying to decide how honest to be.

"I know you've been seeing Bill again," Mrs. Norwood said in a flat, emotionless voice. "I know you've been sneaking out. Is that where you were tonight?"

"Yes," Becka admitted. "How did you know? Did Trish—?"

"It doesn't matter," Mrs. Norwood said sternly.

"Were you listening in on the phone?" Becka demanded.

Her mother frowned. "I don't spy on you," she said, her voice an angry whisper. And then her composure fell apart. "I—I'm just so disappointed in you, Becka," she said, her chin trembling. She chewed her lower lip.

"Mom. Really. I—"

"Sneaking out like that," Mrs. Norwood said, closing her eyes. "Sneaking out behind my back."

"I *had* to sneak out!" Becka snapped. "If I told you I was going to Bill's, you wouldn't let me!"

Mrs. Norwood shook her head sadly. "Becka, Becka. You already had your heart broken once by that boy."

"Mom, that isn't fair!" Becka screamed, advancing on her mother.

Mrs. Norwood, startled by Becka's vehemence, retreated until her back collided with the kitchen table. "Sorry. I didn't mean—"

"Things are different!" Becka screamed, unable to hold her anger, her frustration back. "Bill is different. He's not the same person. But I knew you and Daddy would never believe that. You'd never give Bill a chance."

"So you had to sneak around behind our backs?" Mrs. Norwood demanded, raising her voice to match Becka's.

"What would *you* do?" Becka cried.

"Obey the rules," her mother answered, lowering

her voice, regaining her composure. "That's what I'd do. We have rules in this house, Becka. Important rules about honesty. And you've broken them."

She stared hard at Becka, hands pressed against her waist, one shoe tapping rapidly against the linoleum.

"I—I wanted to tell you about Bill," Becka stammered. "But—"

"But you didn't," her mother said.

Becka could feel herself falling apart.

There was no way she was going to win this argument. No way to get her mom to see her side of the argument.

I can never win an argument against her, Becka realized unhappily. Because she always gets cooler and cooler as the argument continues. And I always fall to pieces and get emotional and lose control.

And that's just what was happening then.

"Mom, you've got to give me a break," Becka pleaded. She crossed her arms in front of her, pressed them tightly against her chest, trying to stop her trembling.

"A break?"

"Yeah. It's hard to explain," Becka started.

"Then don't bother," her mother snapped. She took a deep breath and let it out slowly, staring hard at Becka the whole while.

"Mom, please—"

"Too late," Mrs. Norwood said curtly. "You're grounded."

"Huh?"

"You're grounded. Permanently."

"But, wait. You can't!" Becka cried.

"Oh, yes, I can," Mrs. Norwood said firmly. "I can and I will. You cannot have the car. You cannot see your friends. You cannot go out at night—until further notice."

"But, Mom, it's Christmas vacation," Becka wailed. "What about Trish's party Saturday night?"

"You'll have to miss it," Mrs. Norwood said. She pushed off from the kitchen table and strode quickly from the room.

chapter
19

*B*ecka ran upstairs and threw herself face down on her bed.

She was prepared to cry. She expected the loud sobs to shake her chest and hot tears to fall down her face.

But the tears didn't come. She lay there, her face buried in the bedspread. Too angry to cry. Angry at her mother. Angry at herself. Angry at Bill. She had risked so much by going to see him. And he hadn't been helpful at all.

He hadn't made her feel better. In fact, he had upset her even more by admitting that he thought Honey was "kind of cute" and that "maybe" Honey had come on to him.

Thanks, Bill. Thanks a bunch, Becka thought bitterly.

Now she was angry at Bill too.

Angry at the world.

But still the tears wouldn't come.

She turned her head, pressed the side of her face

against the smooth bedspread, and stared into the darkness.

Now what am I going to do? she thought bitterly.

Some great vacation this is going to be.

She had already laid out her clothes for Trish's party. The short, silver skirt from that little shop in the Old Village. The sleek black catsuit to wear under it.

It was all waiting, ready, set out on the chair in front of her dressing table.

Merry Christmas to me, she thought miserably.

And to all, a good night.

Still the tears wouldn't come.

There was a chill in the room. A sudden waft of cold air.

Had someone left her bedroom window open?

Becka sat up and turned toward the window.

And realized there was someone in the room with her.

chapter
20

The closet door inched open.

A dark figure moved toward the bed.

Silently. Slowly. As if floating.

I'm imagining this, Becka thought, staring into the darkness.

She pulled herself up and started to reach across the bed to click on the lamp.

But a hand shot out and stopped Becka's arm.

"Hey!" Becka cried.

"Ssshhhh. It's me," a voice whispered.

A familiar voice.

Becka squirmed away and fumbled with the lamp.

Finally the light flickered on.

"Honey!" Becka cried.

Leaning out of the shadows, Honey grinned at her mischievously, one finger raised to her lips, a gesture for silence.

"Honey, how did you get in? What are you doing here?" Becka demanded in a loud whisper.

This can't be happening, Becka thought. Honey hasn't moved in? Has she? Has she moved into my room? Is she taking over my entire life?

"Sssshhhhh," Honey repeated.

Becka scooted back across the bedspread until her back was pressed against the headboard. Honey stepped forward until she was inches from the bed.

Her gray eyes sparkled in the harsh lamplight. Her features were twisted in excitement. She was breathing hard.

"How did you get in?" Becka repeated. She stared warily into Honey's glowing eyes, unable to decide if she should be angry or afraid.

"I came to see you earlier," Honey whispered. "Your mother said you were out." Her smile widened.

Becka waited impatiently for her to continue.

"Your mother thought I went home," Honey confided. "I slammed the back door so she'd think I'd left. Then I came up here to wait for you."

"But, Honey," Becka started.

"Just like when we were kids," Honey interrupted. "Remember that time our parents were searching and searching for us? They thought we were outside, but all the time we were hiding in your attic closet?"

"I don't have an attic closet," Becka whispered wearily.

Honey didn't seem to hear her. "I've been waiting a long time for you to get home," she said, assuming a scolding tone.

"But why?" Becka demanded. "Why are you here?"

"I wanted to apologize in person," Honey said, her eyes locked on Becka's, her smile fading.

"Huh? Apologize?"

"Yeah." Honey nodded, her short auburn hair

catching the light. "I felt really bad. It just slipped out, Becka. I'm really sorry."

"Slipped out?"

"About Bill," Honey said, staring intently at Becka, not blinking.

Becka groaned. "I get it. Now, I get it." She slapped both hands against the bedspread.

"Becka, I really—"

"*You* told my mom about Bill," Becka said, forgetting to whisper. "You were the one."

Honey swallowed hard. "It just slipped out."

Now I get it, Becka thought angrily, turning her head to the window. Now I understand. This was Honey's way of paying me back. This was how she paid me back for the scene in the girls' room this afternoon.

She told my mom about Bill.

"I see," Becka muttered keeping her eyes on the window.

"Really," Honey insisted. "It wasn't intentional. Your mother and I were talking, and it just slipped out."

Yeah. Sure, Becka thought, feeling her anger tighten her throat.

"I'm so sorry, Becka. Really. I'm so sorry." She reached forward and tried to wrap Becka in a hug. But Becka pulled back out of her reach.

Honey straightened up stiffly, breathing hard. "Please say you'll forgive me," she begged. "Please."

Becka remained silent, avoiding Honey's eyes.

"Please," Honey pleaded with growing desperation. "Forgive me. You can forgive your best friend, right?"

Becka turned to Honey, her expression hard and

cold. "You're not my friend, Honey," she said through clenched teeth.

Honey jumped back as if she had been slapped. "Huh?"

"You're not my best friend," Becka said, her voice trembling with rage. "You're not my best friend and you're not my friend. Trish and Lilah are my friends. Trish and Lilah are my best friends. My *only* friends."

Honey stared at Becka thoughtfully, as if she were weighing Becka's words carefully.

But her face revealed no emotion at all.

And when she finally spoke, her tone was bright and cheerful, as if she hadn't heard Becka's hurtful words.

"Oh. By the way," Honey said, winking at Becka. "I broke up with Eric today. Just like you did."

"*B*ecka, you're here!"

Trish came hurrying across the crowded living room, pushing her way past groups of chattering, laughing kids.

"Hi, the place looks great!" Becka gazed around the room. A glowing fire cast soft orange light from the fireplace. Large stockings filled with candy canes hung down from the mantel beneath a beautiful Christmas wreath of pine boughs and cones.

An enormous Christmas tree, which touched the ceiling, shimmered in the corner. Its red and white lights twinkled on and off. Dozens of red ribbon bows were tied all along the branches. Silver tinsel made the tree glitter as if it were draped with thousands of sparkling diamonds.

Gazing quickly around the room, Becka recognized many of the smiling, talking faces. What a mob scene! Trish really had invited half the school!

"I really didn't think you'd be able to come," Trish said, shouting over the roar of voices and the blare of music from the stereo, some sort of old school Christmas album.

"My dad gave in at the last minute," Becka told her, grinning. "He talked my mom into letting me come. You look great!"

Trish was wearing a scoop-necked green wool sweater over velvety black pants.

"Great sweater," Becka told her.

"Did you finish yours?" Trish asked. "You know. The one you were knitting for your cousin."

"Oh, sure," Becka said, making a face. "I've had plenty of time to knit since I'm not allowed to go anywhere."

Becka slipped out of her jacket. Trish took it from her, admiring her outfit. Becka was wearing the silver skirt over the black catsuit.

"You look awesome," Trish exclaimed.

Becka smiled and thanked her.

"I'm just throwing all the coats on my parents' bed," Trish said, shouting.

"What is this music?" Becka shouted back. "I really don't believe it!"

"I think it's the Guns 'n Roses Christmas album," Trish replied, laughing. "Gary Brandt brought it. It isn't mine."

Becka took a deep breath. "Mmmmm. What smells so good?"

"Hot apple cider," Trish said. "Go get some." She pointed to the table near the dining room. "It's such a cold, nasty night."

"It's nice and warm in here," Becka said, glancing around the room. "Is Bill here yet?"

"Yeah. I think I saw him in the den. With David Metcalf and some guys."

Trish hurried off with Becka's jacket.

Becka made her way through the room. She poured herself a cup of hot cider, then stopped to talk with Lisa Blume, who was clinging cozily to a red-haired boy Becka didn't know.

Someone changed the CD on the stereo. Suddenly Bruce Springsteen was singing "Santa Claus is Coming to Town."

Becka heard Ricky Schorr complaining to Trish that there was no beer. "How can you have a Christmas party without beer?" he kept asking.

Someone asked Trish where the mistletoe was hung. Trish pointed to the top of the doorframe over the dining room. Ricky told a crude joke about kissing that made everyone groan.

Eager to see Bill, Becka headed to the den. Deena Martinson stopped her just outside the door. "I love that skirt, Becka," she said, taking Becka by the shoulders and making her turn around. "So sexy. I've never seen one like it."

Becka thanked her.

"It looks like wrapping paper almost. Have you seen Jade?" Deena asked, gazing over Becka's shoulder. Jade was Deena's best friend. "I have her keys."

"I don't think she's here yet," Becka replied.

"You look great," Deena repeated. "I heard you were—uh, sick or something."

"No. I'm fine," Becka said.

Bill poked his head out of the den.

"Talk to you later," Becka told Deena.

She hurried to Bill. "Looking for me?"

"No. Looking for some more cider," Bill teased. "But you'll do."

Becka leaned forward and gave him a quick kiss on the cheek. "This is our big night," she said. "Our only night. So don't blow it.

His expression turned serious. "I'm sorry, Becka. But I brought a date."

She believed him for a second.

But he couldn't keep a straight face. He started to laugh.

She gave him a hard shove. He toppled backward against David Metcalf, who was just leaving the den. David, a Shadyside High wrestler, playfully gripped Bill in an armlock.

They wrestled around a bit before Bill cried "uncle" and David let go. "Lookin' good," David said to Becka, eyeing her up and down, before loping off to the refreshment table.

"Well, at least David seems to appreciate me," Becka told Bill coyly.

"David appreciates anything," Bill replied, grinning. "David appreciates a baloney sandwich!"

"Very funny," Becka grumbled. She led the way to the apple cider.

Suddenly Bill grabbed her from behind, spun her around, and kissed her. Startled, Becka pulled back.

Bill grinned and pointed up at the cluster of mistletoe above their heads.

More Shadyside kids arrived. The party grew louder. Someone turned the music up.

Becka and Bill danced, although there wasn't much room to move around in the crowded living room.

Becka felt happy. "This is the best party ever!" she told Trish. Trish agreed.

Later, Becka and Bill had become separated. Where had he disappeared to? she wondered.

She was making her way to the den when she ran into Honey.

"Honey?" Becka couldn't hide her astonishment.

What is she doing here? Becka asked herself. Honey must have crashed the party. Trish would never invite Honey.

Honey gave Becka a hug, then backed up. "Look," she instructed, grinning and gesturing to her outfit.

Becka gaped in shock.

Honey not only had Becka's hairdo. She was wearing the same silver skirt as Becka, over an identical black catsuit.

Honey's grin grew wider. "Hiya, twin!" she exclaimed gleefully.

chapter

22

"I found that shop in the Old Village," Honey said, shouting over the music. "I got the same skirt. I couldn't believe they had another one!" She beamed happily at Becka.

Becka stared back at her, unable to speak.

Why is she here? Becka asked herself, feeling her anger rise. Why is she wearing my clothes? Why is she doing this to me?

"What do you say, twin?" Honey urged. "You haven't said anything."

I can't take it, Becka thought. I can't take it anymore.

Enough!

"Honey, go away," she said through clenched teeth.

"Huh?" Honey's smile faded. She leaned closer to Becka until they were nearly nose to nose. "I can't hear you, Becka. It's so loud in here."

"Go away," Becka repeated more loudly.

"What?"

Becka heard laughter. She glanced up to see two girls she didn't know pointing in her direction. They were obviously commenting to each other about the identical outfits.

This is supposed to be a great night, Becka thought miserably. But instead, I'm being pointed at. Laughed at. All because of Honey.

Her unhappiness quickly turned to rage. Becka could feel herself losing control, but she didn't care.

"Honey, leave me alone!" she shrieked.

Some couples stopped dancing and turned to see what the fuss was about.

"Becka, please! Calm down," Honey said.

"Go away! Leave me alone!" Becka screamed. "You're not my best friend, Honey. You're not even my friend!"

"Becka, *please!*" Honey pleaded, embarrassed.

But Becka couldn't stop herself.

"You're not my friend! You're not! Trish and Lilah are my friends, not you!"

"Becka, stop!"

"You look ridiculous!" Becka screamed, gesturing with both hands to Honey's outfit. "You look gross! You look—pitiful!"

"Calm down, Becka. Everyone's looking!" Honey begged.

"Go away and I'll calm down. Go away, Honey! Leave me alone! I don't want to see you any more!"

Honey's mouth froze wide open. Her face turned pale.

She started to say something. Stopped. Uttered a loud sob.

Then her expression turned angry. Her face reddened. She whirled around, her silver skirt flaring, and ran to the stairs, pushing people out of her path.

Breathing hard, Becka watched her flee up the stairs. Then she turned away, her features still twisted in anger, her hands still knotted into tight fists.

Voices rose around the room. Nervous laughter. Questions.

"What was *that* about?" a girl asked from nearby.

"I heard she had a breakdown," someone else said in a loud whisper.

"Why are they dressed alike?" Becka heard someone ask.

Someone replied, just out of Becka's hearing. The reply was followed by raucous laughter.

Jokes at my expense, Becka thought miserably, feeling her face grow hot. Honey has turned me into a joke. Everyone's talking about me. Everyone's making fun of me now.

"Who was that other girl?" someone asked.

"Weird," Becka heard someone else say.

She looked for Trish. She wanted to apologize for interrupting the party. But Trish was nowhere to be seen.

The music started again, a Christmas rap song. People started dancing. Becka moved to get out of the way.

Her eyes searched the room for Bill. Where has he gone? she wondered. Didn't he hear me yelling at Honey? Is he still in the den?

As she searched for him, her eye caught Trish at the top of the stairs.

What was that Trish was holding?

Squinting to see to the top of the stairs, Becka saw

that Trish was carrying a large Christmas yule log cake on a silver tray.

She saw Trish take a step.

Then she saw that Honey was at the top of the stairs, too. Right behind Trish.

Trish took another step.

And then the enormous cake appeared to fly off the tray.

It took Becka a brief moment to realize that Trish was falling, toppling headfirst down the steep stairs.

A piercing shriek escaped Trish. The horrifying sound followed her all the way down.

The tray hit first, clattering loudly on the hardwood floor.

And then Trish landed with a sickening *crack*.

chapter

23

A frightening silence.

Everyone seemed to freeze as if caught in a snapshot. A snapshot of horror.

The fire popped noisily in the fireplace.

Someone screamed.

The room came back to life.

Becka was one of the first to scramble across the room to Trish.

Trish had landed face down, her chest on top of the cake. The dark icing and cream filling had splattered out across the floor.

Trish didn't move. Her eyes were closed. Her head was tilted at a peculiar angle.

Becka raised her hands to her face, trying to stifle a scream.

Voices rang out. Frightened voices.

"Is she breathing?"

"Don't move her!"

"Is she awake?"

"How did she fall?"

"Someone call nine one one!"

"Where's the phone?"

"Dave is already calling!"

"Somebody call her parents!"

"Don't move her!"

Her heart pounding, Becka leaned over her unmoving friend. "Trish?" she said, her voice trembling. "Trish, can you hear me?"

Silence.

Becka realized her knees were in the gooey white cake filling. But she didn't care.

Trish's head—it was tilted wrong. It shouldn't be bent like that, she saw.

She had the strong urge to take it in both hands and straighten it.

She had the urge to turn Trish around, to sit her up, to hug her.

"Trish?"

Silence.

Behind her, Becka heard kids crying.

The room filled with confused, frightened voices.

"Did she fall?"

"Is she getting up?"

"Did you call nine one one?"

"Are her parents home? Where are they?"

Several kids clustered around Trish in a tight circle, huddling over her, speaking in hushed, frightened tones.

The fire crackled noisily.

Becka's eyes wandered to the top of the stairs.

Honey!

She was still standing on the landing, gripping the banister with one hand. She hadn't moved. She was staring down at them all, a strange expression on her face.

Honey pushed Trish.

The words flashed into Becka's mind, sending a cold chill down her back.

She stared intently up at Honey.

Yes, Honey pushed Trish.

It took Honey a while to realize that she was being watched.

As soon as she noticed Becka staring up at her, she rearranged her expression and started to descend the stairs. "I tried to catch her," Honey cried, tears suddenly glistening in the corners of her eyes. "I tried. But I wasn't fast enough."

Other kids, huddled around Trish, turned their attention to Honey as she made her way slowly down the stairs, tears running down her cheeks.

"I asked her to let me help carry the tray," Honey told them through her tears. "It was so heavy. But she said she had it. And then I saw her start to fall. I grabbed for her. I really did. If only I had been faster. If only . . ." Her voice trailed off, replaced by a loud sob.

No, Becka thought bitterly. No! You pushed her, Honey. You pushed Trish to get back at me.

You pushed Trish. But have you killed her?

"She's breathing funny." Deena Martinson's voice broke into Becka's thoughts. Becka turned to see that Deena was leaning over Trish, her ear lowered nearly to Trish's face, listening hard.

"But she's breathing?" a girl asked from near the fireplace.

"She's breathing, but it's noisy. Like it's hard for her," Deena reported.

"Where's the ambulance?" someone asked.

"Did you call?"

"I called nine one one," came David Metcalf's voice. "I called right away. They should be here."

"I don't hear any sirens," someone said.

"It's snowing out. Maybe they're having trouble," David offered.

"Do we know where her parents are?" a girl asked.

Becka stared down at Trish's unmoving body. Again, she had the strong urge to turn Trish over, to make her more comfortable.

Trish's entire body shuddered.

Becka cried out. So did several others.

But Trish didn't open her eyes. Her breathing was loud and irregular now.

Suddenly Becka felt an arm around her shoulders.

Expecting to see Bill, she turned.

Honey!

"It'll be okay, Becka," Honey whispered, bringing her face close to Becka's. "It'll be okay. I'm here."

Honey uttered a loud sob. Her face was wet with tears.

Her arm was heavy on Becka's shoulder.

"You still have a friend," Honey whispered. "I'm right here. I won't go away. I'm still here."

"No!" Becka screamed.

Several other kids cried out in surprise.

Becka shoved Honey away and climbed to her feet. "No!"

I have to get away, Becka thought. Away!

She ran blindly to the front door, pulled it open, and burst outside—

Into two black-uniformed police officers.

"Whoa!" one of them cried out, more surprised than Becka.

"Where are you going?" the other one demanded.

Gulping for air, Becka took a step back.

"I—I don't know—" Becka stammered. She retreated into the hallway. Everything was a blur. A frightening, spinning blur.

The two officers, shaking snow off their caps, followed her in.

"What's happened here?" one of them asked.

Becka suddenly felt dizzy, dizzy and weak, too dizzy to stand, too weak to take any more of this.

"She did it!" Becka screamed, pointing a shaky finger at Honey. "Honey pushed her! Honey pushed Trish!"

Becka saw Honey's eyes open wide in shock and disbelief.

And then everything went white, as white as the falling snow.

And then, as Becka fell, everything went black.

chapter
24

*B*ecka opened her eyes.

She blinked several times, waiting for her eyes to adjust to the bright light.

Where am I? she wondered.

She tried to sit up. Her back ached. Her arms felt weak.

Have I been sleeping long? she wondered.

The dresser came into focus. Then her dressing table, cluttered with makeup and assorted junk. Dirty clothes were tossed over the chair in front of it.

I'm in my own bedroom, she realized.

I'm home.

But how?

She heard muted voices nearby. She recognized her mother's voice, a loud whisper.

She didn't recognize the man's voice until his face came into view.

Doctor Klein.

He and her mother were huddled in the doorway,

talking softly, intent, serious expressions on their troubled faces. They both turned toward her as Becka struggled to sit up.

"Well, good morning!" her mother called with false brightness. She hurried over to the bed. Dr. Klein followed right behind her.

"Morning?" Becka yawned. "How did it get to be morning? What day is this?"

"Sunday," Mrs. Norwood said, forcing a smile as she stared down at Becka, studying her. "You've been asleep for quite a while."

"Asleep?"

"Your father and I brought you home from the party," her mother said, chewing her bottom lip.

"Right. The party," Becka said groggily.

Suddenly the horror came back to her, sharp as a knife stab. "Trish, is she—?"

"She broke her neck," Mrs. Norwood said, her voice catching. "But she's alive."

"Oh!" Becka cried out. The ceiling started to tilt. She slumped back on her pillow.

"You've had quite a shock," Dr. Klein said, his voice professionally soft. "A terrible shock."

Becka closed her eyes. "I remember the police, but then . . ."

"You passed out," Dr. Klein said, his narrow, mustached face expressionless. The ceiling light reflected off his balding head. "The shock was too overwhelming, no doubt. You had to escape."

"But you're going to be okay," Becka's mother added quickly, nodding her head for emphasis, as if trying to persuade herself. "Doctor Klein says you're going to be fine."

"I'd like you to get complete rest," the doctor said,

shifting his weight, fiddling with the buttons on his gray, pinstriped vest. "Stay in bed for a few days."

"But I'm not sick," Becka protested.

Dr. Klein started to reply, but the phone on Becka's bedside table rang. Mrs. Norwood quickly picked it up after the first ring.

She turned her back to Becka and muttered a few replies, too low for Becka to hear. Then she replaced the receiver.

"That was Honey," she said, turning back to Becka. "She just wondered how you were feeling. She's been calling all morning."

"Nooooo!" Becka uttered a long, painful howl.

Dr. Klein moved quickly to the bed, his face filled with concern. "Are you okay? Does something hurt?"

"Don't let Honey call!" Becka wailed, gripping her sheet with both hands. "I won't talk to her! *I won't!*"

"I hung up. See?" Mrs. Norwood protested, pointing to the phone. She raised her eyes to the doctor, as if asking him to step in.

"As you can see," Dr. Klein began slowly, "you are still very troubled by what took place at the party."

"Don't let Honey call!" Becka interrupted.

"Okay, I'll tell her not to call," her mother replied, her eyes on the doctor.

"No calls," Dr. Klein agreed. "I think that's a good idea, Becka. No calls. Just complete rest. You can go downstairs for meals if you feel like it. You want to get some exercise. You don't want to let yourself get too weak. But don't go out. Don't see anyone. I'm going to prescribe some pills to help relax you."

"Pills?"

"Mild tranquilizers," he said. He picked up his bag.

"You think I'm *crazy?*" The words tumbled out of Becka's mouth.

"Of course not!" Mrs. Norwood immediately protested.

"I think you've been through something really terrifying," Dr. Klein said thoughtfully. "Speaking frankly, which is what we doctors are supposed to do these days, I think you're in a mild state of shock. I think a few days of total rest will probably see you getting back to normal."

Mrs. Norwood followed him to the door.

"I'll check back tomorrow," he said. "Call the office if you need anything at all."

Becka heard him clomp down the stairs. A short while later, her mother returned, nervously pushing back a strand of hair from her forehead, a forced smile on her face. "You'll be fine," she said, smoothing her hand over Becka's forehead. "Feel like eating anything? I could bring you up something on a tray."

Becka shook her head. "No thanks, Mom. I feel kind of sleepy, actually."

Becka drifted into a deep sleep.

For the next few days she drifted in and out of consciousness, spending very little time awake. Her sleep was deep and dreamless, and she awoke feeling tired and not at all refreshed.

One evening her mother entered to find Becka sitting up in bed, crying about Trish, tears rolling down her cheeks, dropping onto her coverlet.

"That's it," Mrs. Norwood said softly, tenderly placing a hand on Becka's shoulder. "Let it out. Let those feelings out, dear. Then you'll feel better."

Becka cried and cried. She cried till she had no tears left, but she didn't feel better.

The next afternoon found her feeling a little stronger. Her appetite had returned, and she had eaten an enormous lunch.

She had talked to both Trish and Lilah on the phone. Her friends were in the same wing of Shadyside General, almost across the hall from each other. Lilah sounded bored, eager to get out. It was taking a long time for her shattered leg to heal. Trish sounded weak. And very depressed. She had told Becka that she had no memory of what had happened —one moment she was at the top of the stairs, the next, she was in the hospital. As Trish talked, Becka could hear the pain in her voice. If only there was something I could do to stop this nightmare, thought Becka, feeling alone and helpless.

Becka promised to go see them as soon as she was allowed.

Later that afternoon she was back in bed, reading a book, the radio on low in the background, when her mother entered, dressed to go out. "I'll be back in less than an hour," she said, fretfully pulling at a glove. "You'll be okay, won't you?"

"Of course," Becka told her. "No problem."

"How do you feel?" Mrs. Norwood asked. She asked the question twenty times a day.

"Kind of sleepy," Becka admitted. "I didn't think it was possible for a person to sleep so much!"

Becka said it lightly, but her mother's fretful expression turned more serious. "It's good for you," she said. "I'll be right back, okay? You stay in bed. Go back to sleep."

"Don't worry about me," Becka said, yawning.

She closed the book and let it drop to the floor. Yawning, she listened to her mother pad down the stairs. A few seconds later the front door slammed. A few seconds after that Becka heard the car start up and back down the drive.

Suddenly Becka felt a wave of sadness sweep over her.

It's the pills, she thought.

The pills are depressing me, making me feel sad.

No, she argued with herself. It's not the pills. It's me. It's my life. My life is so sad. So very, very sad.

"Where are my friends?" she cried aloud, feeling herself start to tremble.

"Where are my friends?"

All hurt. All in the hospital.

All gone.

She pulled the covers up to her chin.

Feeling so sad. Feeling sleepy. And heavy, as if she weighed a thousand pounds. And shaky.

And sad.

And just as she was drifting into another deep sleep, the phone rang.

chapter

25

"No phone calls." Becka heard Dr. Klein's words.

The phone rang a second time.

Don't answer it, she thought. I'm too sad to answer it.

A third ring.

She wondered why her mother didn't pick it up.

Then she remembered her mother had gone out.

I'm not thinking too clearly, Becka realized. I'm too sad to think clearly.

A fourth ring, jangling loudly in Becka's ear.

She picked up the receiver. "Hello?" Her voice escaped, soft and timid.

"Hi, Becka, is that you? It's Honey."

"Oh." She uttered the word wearily, not surprised.

I'm too sad to talk to you, Honey. I'm too sad because of you.

"I've been thinking about you," Honey said cheerily.

Becka didn't reply. The phone receiver felt so heavy in her hand.

Why am I holding on to it? she asked herself. Why don't I just drop it back down?

I'm not thinking clearly at all.

"Becka, are you still there?" Honey asked impatiently.

"Yeah."

"You weren't very nice to me, Becka. Not very nice at all. But I have a nice surprise for you," Honey said, giggling.

Why is she so happy? Becka wondered grudgingly.

She felt cold all over, cold and trembly. And so sad. Why is Honey so happy while I'm so sad?

"Can you come over?" Honey asked eagerly.

"Huh?"

"Come over," Honey urged. "Just for a second. Just to see the nice surprise I have. You'll like it, Becka. Really."

"No," Becka told her. The room tilted and swayed. She shut her eyes to make it stop. "No, I can't."

"You have to," Honey insisted. "You'll like this surprise, Becka. Put on your coat. Run over for just a second. You'll be glad. Really."

No.

I can't.

I'm too sad. Too sleepy, Too heavy.

I can't.

As Honey pleaded with her to come over, Becka heard another voice in the background. A boy's voice.

Bill?

Was that Bill she heard? Was Bill over at Honey's? *Why?*

"Please. Hurry," Honey urged.

"Okay," she told Honey. "Okay. I'll come. Just this once. Just for a minute."

"Oh, good!" Honey exclaimed. "I have something to show you. A big surprise!"

As if in a trance, Becka lifted herself from her bed. The room tilted and swayed.

She held on to the dressertop to steady herself.

Her heart pounded. "It wasn't Bill," she said aloud. "It couldn't be Bill. I imagined Bill's voice. Bill would never go to Honey's house."

But she had to make sure.

I'm only staying a second, she thought.

I told Honey. Only a second.

And then I'm never seeing her again. Never talking to her again.

She pulled on her terrycloth robe. Then slipped into her sneakers.

No need to get dressed, she thought.

I'm only going out for a second.

She peeked out the window. Snow covered the ground. The late afternoon sky was charcoal gray. Threatening clouds hovered low over the rooftops. The snow appeared shiny and hard as ice.

It's been on the ground a long time, Becka thought, staring down at it.

I haven't looked outside all week.

Isn't that strange? I haven't seen the sky. Haven't seen the snow. Haven't looked outside even once?

What's *wrong* with me? she wondered.

Why do I feel so strange?

Why don't I feel like me?

She made her way unsteadily down the stairs and stopped at the front closet to get her coat. Then, slipping it over her shoulders, pulling the drawstring of her robe, she headed to the back door.

It was colder outside than she had imagined. Becka zipped up the coat and, bending into the wind, made her way over the hard, slippery snow.

She crossed her backyard behind the garage, stepped between an opening in the scraggly hedge, and entered Honey's backyard.

Shivering, she hurried toward the back door.

She stopped a few yards from the house as two figures came into sharp focus through the kitchen window.

"No!" Becka screamed in horror. "Oh, *no!"*

chapter
26

A thin layer of frost covered Honey's kitchen window. But the bright light inside the kitchen allowed Becka a clear view of the two people seated at the yellow Formica table.

Standing in the snow, her sneakers unlaced, her trembling hands bare, Becka gaped at them open-mouthed.

There was Honey, smiling across the table. Wearing Becka's hairdo.

Taking a step closer, Becka recognized her best green sweater on Honey, with the enamel parrot pin at the neck.

And sitting across from Honey, smiling warmly across the table, was Bill.

Were they holding hands?

Becka couldn't see.

Something snapped in Becka's mind.

Everything went white, as white as the ice-hard snow at her feet.

Everything went cold, as cold as the wind that tried to push her away from the back door.

But Becka refused to be pushed away.

"She can't have Bill too!" she shrieked against the wind. The words burst out in an angry, high-pitched wail.

She's taken everything from me, Becka thought bitterly, seized with fury. Everything. But she can't take Bill. She can't!

Her eyes blurred by hot tears, Becka grabbed the knob on the back door, turned it and pushed.

Panting loudly, she burst into the bright kitchen.

Panting. Panting like an angry animal, she glared at them.

Sitting there together. The two of them. Smiling.

Together in the bright, warm kitchen.

"No!" Becka wailed.

Her eyes searched frantically for something. She didn't know what.

Something.

There it was. The wooden knife holder on the counter.

The wooden knife holder with the large, black-handled kitchen knives.

"Becka," surprise!" Honey called gleefully, gesturing to Bill.

She started to get up from the table, but stopped halfway when she saw Becka pull the knife from the holder.

The blade glistened in the bright kitchen light.

Bill's smile faded quickly. His eyes opened wide with surprise.

Honey remained frozen, half in the chair, half out.

"Becka, what—?" Honey didn't finish her sentence.

She swallowed hard, then uttered a frightened cry of protest as Becka raised the knife high.

"No, Becka, stop!"

But Becka was screaming too loud to hear her, screaming as she flew across the room, screaming out her fury as she lunged toward Honey with the knife aimed at Honey's chest.

chapter
27

*K*ill, Becka thought.

I'm going to kill Honey.

I *have* to kill her. Kill her. *Kill her!*

Then I'll be happy again. So happy.

But halfway across the kitchen floor, Becka stopped short.

The whirling, tilting room dimmed to black.

She uttered a low groan.

Weak. I feel so weak. I feel so totally weak.

Her eyes rolled up, and she slumped to the floor.

She hit the floor hard and didn't move.

She didn't see the knife bounce out of her hand.

She didn't see Bill jump up from the table. "You *told* me Becka knew I was here!" he shouted angrily at Honey. "You told me she was coming over to see me!"

He moved quickly to see if he could help Becka, but Honey pulled him back.

"Stay away from her!" she cried, her eyes wild with excitement. "She's *my* friend!"

"Are you *crazy?*" Bill shouted, wrenching out of Honey's grasp. "She's fainted. She might've hurt herself. We have to do something!"

"Stay away!" Honey repeated, her voice lowering with menace. "She's my friend. My *best* friend."

Becka groaned but didn't awaken.

Her large hand trembling, Honey picked up the big kitchen knife from where it had landed on the floor near the counter. Standing over Becka's unmoving body, she threatened Bill with it.

"You're crazy!" he cried, fear mixing suddenly with the anger in his voice. "Put that down. What are you doing?"

"Stay away from my best friend," Honey instructed him, her features twisted in ugly fury.

With a rapid swipe of his arm, Bill made a grab for the knife.

He grabbed onto the handle just above Honey's hand.

"Let go!" she screamed.

"Drop it, Honey!"

They wrestled for only a moment.

Honey bumped him away with her shoulder.

As he stumbled back, he made a desperate attempt to hold onto the knife.

But Honey had it now.

Catching his balance, Bill surged forward, reaching, reaching for it—and tumbled into the knife.

The blade pierced his chest.

Startled, Honey uttered a shrill cry.

It took her a few seconds to pull the knife out.

A bright circle of blood spread across the front of Bill's sweatshirt.

"Hey," he rasped, his voice a hoarse whisper. A loud, sickening gurgle escaped his open lips. "I'm—cut." He raised his eyes to Honey's and they revealed his disbelief, his horror.

He groaned, then slumped facedown beside Becka onto the linoleum. The blood puddled around him, spreading out over the floor.

He's dead, Honey realized.

He's dead and his blood is so bright.

Becka stirred. She groaned. Her entire body shuddered.

Honey forced her eyes away from the blood flowing around Bill.

Now what? Honey thought, her heart pounding.

Now what? Now what? Now what?

Her eyes darted frantically from Becka to Bill, then back to Becka.

Suddenly she had an idea.

She bent down over Becka.

She placed the knife in Becka's hand.

She carefully wrapped Becka's fingers around the black handle.

Honey stood up and stared at the blood-stained knife now held tightly in Becka's hand.

After a few seconds Becka opened her eyes. Honey dropped down beside her and helped her sit up.

"Don't worry," Honey whispered in Becka's ear. "Don't worry, Becka."

She cradled Becka in her arms.

Groggily, Becka squinted and tried to focus. But she could see only lights, bright, shimmery lights.

The room was a glimmering blur.

What was happening? Why couldn't she get it in focus?

"Don't worry," Honey repeated gently. "I'll take care of you, Becka. I'm your only friend now. I'll take care of you."

Becka struggled to see clearly.

She uttered a silent gasp when she saw the knife in her hand.

Slowly her eyes began to focus.

Becka saw the blood-soaked blade. Red and silver. Red and silver. It glistened like a shiny Christmas tree ornament.

Everything was glistening, sparkling in the light. The red and silver knife in her hand. The kitchen counters. The boy lying facedown beside her . . .

"I'll take care of you, Becka," Honey whispered soothingly, holding on to Becka. "I won't let the police know what you did. We'll make up a story, won't we, Becka? We won't let them know that you murdered Bill."

"Huh?" Becka struggled to get up, but Honey held on, keeping her arms around Becka's shoulders, whispering soothingly in her ear.

"What did I do?" Becka whispered. "What?"

She stared at the red and silver knife in her hand.

Then she lowered her gaze to Bill, lying so still in a dark puddle of blood.

"What did I do?" Becka whispered.

"I'll tell them you did it in self-defense, Becka," Honey said softly. "They won't have to know the truth. They'll never know you stabbed Bill. Because I'll protect you. I'll protect you from now on. Because I'm your best friend. I'm your best friend, and I'm your only friend, aren't I. Becka? Aren't I? Aren't I your best friend? *Aren't* I? Of course I am. I'm your best best friend. And I will never let them know what you did to Bill. Never. Never *never.*"

"Thank you, Honey," Becka whispered gratefully.

About the Author

R.L. Stine invented the teen horror genre with Fear Street, the bestselling teen horror series of all time. He also changed the face of children's publishing with the mega-successful Goosebumps series, which *Guinness World Records* cites as the Best-Selling Children's Book Series ever, and went on to become a worldwide multimedia phenomenon. The first two books in his new series Mostly Ghostly, *Who Let the Ghosts Out?* and *Have You Met My Ghoulfriend?*, are *New York Times* bestsellers. He's thrilled to be writing for teens again in the brand-new Fear Street Nights books.

R.L. Stine has received numerous awards of recognition, including several Nickelodeon Kids' Choice Awards and Disney Adventures Kids' Choice Awards, and he has been selected by kids as one of their favorite authors in the National Education Association Read Across America. He lives in New York City with his wife, Jane, and their dog, Nadine.

Dear Readers,

Welcome to FEAR STREET—where your worst nightmares live! It's a terrifying place for Shadyside High students—and for YOU!

Did you know that the sun never shines on the old mansions of Fear Street? No birds chirp in the Fear Street woods. And at night, eerie moans and howls ring through the tangled trees.

I've written nearly a hundred Fear Street novels, and I am thrilled that millions of readers have enjoyed all the frights and chills in the books. Wherever I go, kids ask me when I'm going to write a new Fear Street trilogy.

Well, now I have some exciting news. I have written a brand-new Fear Street trilogy. The three new books are called FEAR STREET NIGHTS. The saga of Simon and Angelica Fear and the unspeakable evil they cast over the teenagers of Shadyside will continue in these new books. Yes, Simon and Angelica Fear are back to bring terror to the teens of Shadyside.

FEAR STREET NIGHTS is available now. . . . Don't miss it. I'm very excited to return to Fear Street—and I hope you will be there with me for all the good, scary fun!

RL Stine

The first two novels in the captivating series

wicked

Witch & Curse

Nancy Holder & Debbie Viguié

Witches
Secrets
Alliances
Destiny

A series by
Nancy Holder and
Debbie Viguié

The third and fourth novels in the captivating series

wicked 2

Legacy & Spellbound

Nancy Holder & Debbie Viguié

From Simon Pulse
Published by Simon & Schuster

feel the fear.

FEAR STREET® NIGHTS

A brand-new Fear Street trilogy by the master of horror

R.L. STINE

In Stores Now

Simon Pulse
Published by Simon & Schuster
FEAR STREET is a registered trademark of Parachute Press, Inc.